MW01286610

WISTERIA WEDDING

RACHEL HANNA

CHAPTER 1

Danielle sat in front of her laptop as she did most days, her finger hovering over the trackpad while she waited for her mother to answer a video call. Her heart pounded with a mixture of excitement and nervousness. The weight of the new diamond engagement ring on her left hand still felt a bit unfamiliar, but also exciting. How would her mother react to her engagement? There was no way to predict that.

The screen finally flickered to life, and she saw her mother's perfectly coiffed silver hair and crisp white blazer appear before her. Even though she was a little bit pixelated on the video feed, Cecilia Wright always looked like the most elegant person in the world. She had poise, and her sharp eyes immediately zeroed in on Danielle's face.

"Danielle, darling, to what do I owe the pleasure of this unexpected call?" Her voice had the faintest hint of Southern drawl, which was just a charming remnant of her Atlanta upbringing that even her decades in New York hadn't fully erased.

Danielle sucked in a deep breath, unable to contain the smile spreading across her face. "Mom, I have some huge news. Bennett proposed, and I said yes. We're engaged." She held up her hand, grinning.

Cecilia looked surprised, stunned even. Her perfectly arched eyebrows - that she had done in what she called the "best salon in New York City"- arched upward. Then a smile bloomed, lighting up her elegant features.

"Oh my gosh! Congratulations, sweetheart. I'm so happy for you." She leaned closer to the screen. "Now tell me everything. Exactly how did he propose? Goodness, we have so much planning to do."

As Danielle recounted the proposal to her mother, she could practically see the gears turning in her mother's head. Cecilia had always wanted a big, grand society wedding for her only daughter. While Danielle appreciated her mother's enthusiasm, she felt a knot of anxiety forming in her stomach.

She and Bennett had envisioned a simple, intimate ceremony on Wisteria Island, surrounded by the community they loved so much.

"Actually, Mom, Bennett and I are planning to have the wedding here on the island. You know, it's become the most important place in the world for both of us, and we want to celebrate with our friends here," Danielle began, watching as her mother's expression changed.

Cecilia waved dismissively, her perfectly manicured nails flashing across the screen. "Oh, nonsense, darling. A wedding on that little island with a bunch of retired people? Come on, you deserve a real celebration. You just leave everything to me. I'll book The Plaza and call that amazing wedding planner, Lydia Harrington. She did the wedding for Angelique's oldest daughter, and it was beautiful. Somehow, she made that plain Jane daughter look beautiful, so I know she has some tricks up her sleeve. Oh, and we'll need to fly to Paris for your dress…"

Danielle's heart sank as her mother prattled on about guest lists and color schemes. She should have known her mother would have grand plans that didn't align at all with the intimate island wedding she and Bennett dreamed of. Danielle loved her mother, but their visions for the perfect wedding couldn't be more different.

She braced herself for what she knew would be an uphill battle.

Just then, a knock sounded at the door.

"Oh, Mom, I need to go. We'll talk more later. Love you," Danielle said, ending the call before her mother could say anything else.

She opened the door to find Eddie, the island's jack-of-all-trades, looking uncharacteristically somber.

"Hey, Eddie, what's going on?"

"Oh, sorry to bother you, Dani, but Bennett wanted me to let you know that a new resident has arrived, and she seems a bit lost. He was hoping you might check on her and make sure she's settling in okay."

Danielle nodded, her previous concerns about the wedding momentarily forgotten. Tending to the island's residents always took top priority.

"Oh, of course. Let me go grab my bag, and I'll head over. What's her name?"

"Clara Whitman. Recently widowed, retired

orchestra conductor. Bennett says she's been struggling since her husband passed away."

"Oh, poor thing. I'll see what I can do."

Danielle grabbed her medical bag and pushed thoughts of wedding plans aside as she headed out to welcome the island's newest resident. She was determined to help her however she could.

She walked the short distance to Clara's cottage and spotted a figure slumped in a rocking chair on the front porch. The woman appeared to be in her late sixties, with her silver hair pulled back in a simple ponytail. She wore a plain black dress that hung loosely on her thin frame. Even from a distance, Danielle could see grief emanating from her, a heaviness that seemed to weigh down her tiny shoulders.

Danielle approached slowly, not wanting to startle her.

"Clara, I'm Danielle Wright, the island's nurse. I just wanted to come and see how you're settling in."

Clara looked up. Her dull blue eyes were rimmed with red, evidence of recently shed tears. She tried to smile, but it just came out as a grimace.

"Oh, hello. I'm, um, fine, thank you. Just trying to get my bearings around here, I suppose."

Danielle sat in the chair beside her, sensing that that was far from the truth.

"Listen, Clara, I understand it can be really overwhelming moving to a new place, especially under these difficult circumstances. I'm so sorry for your loss."

At the mention of her husband, Clara's eyes filled with tears. Her lower lip trembled as she tried to maintain her composure.

"Thirty-six years. We had thirty-six wonderful years together. I don't know how I'm going to do life without him."

Danielle reached out, took her hand, and offered a gentle squeeze.

"You're not alone, Clara. These people, this island —well, we all care for each other here. We're family, and I know it doesn't feel like it right now, but you'll find your way again, a new way. Until you do, we'll be here to help you. There are lots of men and women on this island who understand losing a spouse. Please try to make friends and get some support that way, too."

Clara looked at Danielle. "Thank you. I think that I'm going to need a lot of help. Probably more than I realized." She paused for a moment. "So, would you like to come inside?" Clara asked after a few moments. "I mean, I can't offer much. I just moved in. I haven't even unpacked the kitchen yet, but I think I might be able to manage making some tea."

Danielle smiled. "I'd like that very much."

The inside of Clara's cottage showed her grief. There were half-unpacked boxes stacked haphazardly all over the living room, some labeled in a precise masculine hand that had to have been her late husband's, and then a grand piano dominated one corner. Danielle couldn't imagine how they had gotten it onto the island. It was clearly untouched since her arrival, with its polished surface already collecting some dust.

Clara entered the small kitchen, filled a kettle, and set it on the stove. She was performing the movements like it was something she just remembered but no longer enjoyed.

"That piano is beautiful," Danielle said, hoping to start a conversation.

Clara looked over at it. "You know, Robert gave me that on our twentieth anniversary. I haven't been able to bring myself to play it since..." She trailed off, looking at the teacups.

"So, music was a shared passion."

"Oh, it was our life," Clara said, a hint of happiness returning to her voice. "We met during a summer program. I was conducting a youth orchestra. He was the guest conductor for a symphony orchestra. He came to one of my rehearsals and told me he had never seen anyone command a room the way I did. He said my hands spoke a language he'd been trying to learn his whole life."

"Wow, he sounds like a remarkable man," Danielle said.

"Oh, he was. And handsome, Hollywood handsome." The kettle whistled, and Clara poured steaming water into a teapot. "But enough about my troubles. Tell me about this island. It's very different from anywhere I've lived before."

Danielle sat with Clara and told her things about the island. She told her about some of the biggest personalities, like Morty. She told her about the activities they did and how it worked with her being the island nurse. But mostly, she just kept Clara company for as long as she could.

As Danielle sat with Clara, listening as she shared stories of her husband and their beautiful life together, she felt a renewed sense of purpose. This is why she became a nurse - not just to treat people's physical ailments but to provide support, comfort, and even a listening ear when somebody needed it the most.

The wedding planning could wait.

Her most important role right now was to be there for Clara and the other residents of Wisteria Island as they navigated life. Together, they would help Clara heal and find her place among them.

Morty was hunched over his laptop, his reading glasses perched precariously at the end of his nose. The screen's glow lit up his face as he scrolled through page after page, his eyes widening with each new discovery.

"Oh, my stars," he muttered to himself.

He could barely contain his excitement. He had never gotten to do anything like this.

"This is perfect. It's absolutely perfect," he said, throwing up his hands.

On the screen before him was Pinterest, which had turned out to be a virtual treasure trove of wedding inspiration. From color palettes to center-pieces, boutonnieres to bouquets, Morty was deeply in his element. He had taken it upon himself to help plan the wedding of the century for Danielle and Bennett, the two people who had become like family to him on their little island.

"Rustic chic. Oh, no, no, no. That simply will not do. Oh, but this—a beach boho theme," he said, clapping his hands together. "Oh, my goodness! Look at those touches of coastal glam."

Morty was practically bouncing in his seat as his mind raced with ideas. He began feverishly creating Pinterest boards, pinning images of driftwood arbors draped in gauzy fabrics and tables covered in seashells and sand dollars. He imagined barefoot bridesmaids wearing flowy seafoam green dresses. In his mind, this would be unlike any other celebration Wisteria Island had ever seen.

"Oh, my goodness, Danielle is going to love this," he said to himself, grinning so hard that he feared his cheeks would hurt later. "Oh, and Bennett, too. I just can't wait to show them."

Nobody was there, but Morty was accustomed to talking to himself. He'd done it since he was a little kid. And the great thing was, he always agreed with what he said.

He knew some people might find his enthusiasm a bit much, but he couldn't help it. He'd never had the chance to plan a wedding before, let alone for the two people that he cared about so deeply. This was his chance to show Danielle and Bennett just how much they meant to him and the whole island community.

A knock at the door interrupted Morty's planning frenzy. He pushed his laptop aside and walked to the door, still muttering something about fairy lights to himself.

"Oh, Janice, what a wonderful surprise," he said, finding the pink-haired square dancer on his doorstep.

"Good evening, Morty. I saw your lights on and thought I'd drop by for a bit. Good lord, what's got you all worked up? I could hear you talking to yourself from the sidewalk."

Morty pulled her inside, unable to contain his excitement. "I'm planning Danielle and Bennett's wedding. It's going to be spectacular. Beach ceremony at sunset, reception under the stars, I might even create a dance floor right there on the sand—but don't tell them, they don't know anything about it."

Janice's eyes lit up. "Oh, a wedding, how wonderful. You know, I used to be a florist before I retired. I made arrangements for more than a hundred weddings back in my day."

"You did? Oh, Janice, then you have to help me. I was thinking about using local wildflowers with touches of wisteria, but I'm not sure about the logistics of that."

He trailed off, and then the two friends huddled over Morty's laptop, discussing boutonnieres and table centerpieces. He needed all the help he could get, but he didn't want Danielle and Bennett to know anything about his plans.

After a bit, Janice had to leave to go to square dance practice, and Morty got back to it.

He continued to plan and pin things as his heart swelled with joy and excitement. The wedding was weeks away at least, but he knew that with a little creativity and a lot of love—and maybe a few sequins, because honestly, why not?—it would be a day that none of them would ever forget.

As the sun began to set over Wisteria Island, he looked out over the beach and thought about the wedding day filled with joy, laughter, tears, and probably more than a few unexpected twists and turns. But the one thing that he was certain of - that on their little island, love and friendship would always find a way to shine through.

B ennett stood on the deck of his cottage, watching as the sunrise painted the sky in beautiful shades of pink and orange. The waves lapped at the shore, as they always did, providing a soothing soundtrack to his morning coffee ritual.

He couldn't help but smile as he thought about his recent engagement to Danielle.

"Engaged," he whispered to himself, still hardly believing it.

He had assumed he might be a lifelong bachelor after so many years of not finding the right person to spend his life with, but Danielle was definitely that person. After all, her name was *Miss Wright*. Every time he thought about it, it made him laugh.

His phone buzzed in his pocket, and he pulled it out. Naomi's name flashed across the screen.

"Good morning, Naomi. You're up bright and early."

"Good morning," she said. "I just wanted to confirm that you're still available for that budget meeting at nine. Oh, and I've also scheduled some interviews with three potential temporary nurses for next week. You know Danielle's going to need coverage during your honeymoon, so I assume you still plan on whisking her away to parts unknown?"

He laughed. "Yes, to all of the above, although I'm

starting to think I should just close the island for two weeks and take everybody on a vacation."

"Well, that would certainly be easier than finding someone willing to step into Danielle's very hard-to-fill shoes, even temporarily," Naomi said. "Oh, also, Morty has requested a - and I quote - *urgent meeting* with you about wedding plans. Those were his words, not mine, but he seemed very enthusiastic."

Bennett groaned. "I can't remember a time Morty wasn't enthusiastic. Tell him I'll stop by his place after the budget meeting."

After ending the call, Bennett took another sip of his coffee and let his mind wander to thoughts of Clara Whitman, the island's newest resident. It always surprised him how much he cared about everyone living on the island. The moment they moved there, they became like family. He worried over them like they were his kids—or more like it, his grandparents.

Danielle had texted him last night after spending hours with the grieving widow. She was clearly struggling, so Bennett made a mental note to check on her himself later in the day.

One of the things he loved most about Danielle was her immense compassion. Where others might have just seen a sad woman, she saw her pain—saw someone who needed support, someone to sit with her and listen. Danielle offered the residents so much more than just medical treatment. She offered friendship. She offered a listening ear, and the same compassion had won over even the most stubborn residents of Wisteria Island, like Dorothy and Ted.

Bennett finished his coffee and then headed inside to prepare for the day. He couldn't help but keep a smile on his face as he got dressed and tidied up the cottage before leaving.

Today would be just another day on Wisteria Island, but in the back of his mind, he couldn't help looking forward to the day he would stand before an officiant and marry the love of his life.

CHAPTER 2

Clara Whitman sat at her weathered kitchen table, looking at the unpacked boxes stacked against the wall. After thirty-six years of marriage, she had certainly accumulated a lifetime of memories, but they were all now condensed into sad cardboard containers labeled with her husband's neat handwriting.

"Kitchen – Fragile," one box read.

Her Robert had always been so organized, so methodical. He would have had this cottage unpacked and arranged in less than a day, but she'd been here for nearly a week and had barely even managed to unpack her clothes. She just couldn't seem to force herself to do it.

She reached for the framed photograph beside

her - a picture of her beloved Robert conducting the symphony orchestra, his face full of passion, his arms raised up in mid-gesture. That's how she always wanted to remember him: as this person who was so vibrant and alive, not as she'd seen him in the final days of his life, so withered and weak from cancer that claimed him far too soon.

They had met a little later in their lives and never had children—something that bothered Clara even today. Oh, how she wished she had a big family. How she wished she had kids and grandkids and was simply waiting for great-grandkids. She wished she lived on some big property somewhere where all her kids and grandkids would gather around her and have big Sunday dinners. She sometimes dreamed of sitting on her front porch on some big piece of land, watching one of her grandkids run toward her with arms open wide.

But now she lived on a tiny island with a bunch of other people who either didn't have families that wanted them around or just needed a place to go in their older years that didn't reek of lemon-scented cleaner and sadness.

She'd quickly learned that Wisteria Island was full of the same kinds of people. There were the people who wanted to be there. Some people needed to be there, like her, simply because they had nowhere else to go. And then there were the people whose families had sent them there because they didn't want to deal with them, because they were too eccentric or problematic.

It sometimes seemed times had changed a lot from when she was a kid. Back when elders were revered instead of ignored. Back when their wisdom was important to younger generations. Or maybe she was just wallowing in self-pity and anger that her life had been so destroyed by the death of her husband. Her best friend. The rock she'd held onto for so many years. She felt adrift now, like a tiny leaf in the wide open ocean.

She was thankful that she'd had the choice and the funds to come to a place like this, to grow old with people around her to care for her, at least in some way. She was thankful the island had a nurse, and she had people who might become her friends one day.

But right now, she was so stuck in her grief that she didn't know when that could happen.

A knock at the door startled her.

"Mrs. Whitman, it's Bennett Alexander. I hope I'm not disturbing you," she heard him say from the other side of the door.

She quickly wiped away a stray tear and smoothed her hair before opening the door.

"Mr. Alexander, please do come in. And you can call me Clara."

"Well, only if you'll call me Bennett," he said, smiling as he stepped into the cottage. "I just wanted to see how you're settling in. Danielle mentioned that you might need some help unpacking. I can certainly come over here after work."

Clara felt a rush of embarrassment. "I'm afraid I've been a little slow to get organized," she said, forcing a smile.

Bennett seemed very kind, with no trace of judgment.

"You know, grief moves at its own pace, Clara. There's no timeline you have to follow. Many of the people on this island have experienced grief, just like you have." He looked around the cottage. "But you know, if you want some help, we have a bunch of volunteers here who can help you get settled. They'll be efficient and understanding, I promise."

Clara hesitated, feeling her natural independence bubbling up to the surface. But it was at war with the overwhelming fatigue that had been her constant companion since losing the love of her life.

"You know, I…" she said, trailing off. "Actually, that would be very kind. Thank you."

Bennett nodded. "Consider it done. I understand you've been in the world of music for a long time?"

"Yes. Robert and I actually met when we were both conducting. I was a rare female conductor, so I stood out like a sore thumb. We both played instruments as well, but mostly piano."

"Music has always been a real passion of mine, though I lack any real talent," Bennett said, laughing. "We do have a small music program here on the island. It's nothing fancy, but some residents get together and play. They've been looking for someone with experience to guide them."

She felt a flicker of interest for the first time in months. "Really? What sort of ensemble?"

"Well, they're quite a motley crew, to be honest. I think we have a violinist, a cellist, a clarinetist, and a very enthusiastic but somewhat unorthodox pianist. They call themselves the Wisteria Philharmonic, which seems a little ambitious given their number."

Clara found a small smile forming on her face. "That sounds interesting."

"Well, they meet on Thursday afternoons at the community center. There's no pressure at all, but if you want to, go ahead and stop by, even if it's just to listen."

When he left a few minutes later, Clara stood at the window watching him walk down the sidewalk. She felt a little spark of possibility for the first time since she arrived on the island.

Maybe there was still some music left in her life after all.

Danielle finished examining Gladys's blood pressure and then smiled. "You're looking good, Gladys. That medication change is working really well."

"Oh, thank goodness. I was worried I would have to give up my pickle addiction," Gladys said, rolling down her sleeve.

"Well, moderation is still key," Danielle reminded her. "But yes, your numbers are much better than last month."

She made notes in Gladys's chart as her phone buzzed with a text from her mother. She quickly glanced at it.

Called several venues in New York.
The Plaza is available June 15th.
Perfect timing for a summer
wedding. Sending you their brochure
and pricing. XOXO, Mom.

Danielle sighed and put the phone aside without saying anything or responding to her mother.

"Wedding troubles already?" Gladys asked. As irreverent as Gladys could be, she was perceptive.

"My mother has some ideas about what my wedding should be like."

"Oh, I see. And they don't match yours?"

Danielle smiled. "Not even close. She wants this big, grand New York City society affair, and I want a simple beach ceremony right here on the island."

Gladys patted her hand. "Oh, mothers and daughters. Always complicated relationships. Well, my own mother insisted I wear *her* wedding gown. A monstrosity of satin and lace that made me look like a walking meringue."

"Did you wear it?"

"Oh, good Lord, no. I *accidentally*" - she used air quotes - "spilled red wine all over it two weeks before the wedding." Gladys winked mischievously. "Sometimes you must be a little crafty to get your way."

Danielle laughed. "Well, I'm not sure sabotage is exactly the answer, but I think I need to start being more firm with my mom."

"You just remember this, dear. It's *your* day. It's not hers. And that handsome man of yours only has eyes for you, whether you're in a fancy gown at The Plaza or barefoot out there on the beach. Just watch out for those jellyfish that keep washing up."

After Gladys left, Danielle looked at her schedule and saw she had a short break before her next patient. She would use that time to call her mother to establish boundaries. But just as she was about to dial, there was a knock at her office door, and then Morty entered in his normal flamboyant way.

"Oh, Danielle, darling, I have the most *fabulous* news."

He looked like he was practically vibrating with excitement as he clutched a tablet to his chest. Of course, Danielle couldn't take her eyes off his hot pink golf shirt and his brightly striped knee shorts. Sometimes, she needed sunglasses to look at him.

"What's up, Morty?"

"I've been working on your wedding plans. Now, before you say anything, look at what I've put together," he said, holding up his hands.

He thrust the tablet into her hands, revealing a

meticulously organized Pinterest board titled **Beach Boho Glam Wedding Extravaganza**. Danielle scrolled through the images and was surprised to find that many of them actually aligned with what she'd envisioned—a simple ceremony on the beach with natural decorations that had elegance, and then a big reception under the stars.

"Morty, this is beautiful despite the title that goes a little over the top. And way fewer sequins than I would think."

He beamed with pride. "I just knew you'd love it. I've already spoken to Esther at the bakery about the cake. She's thinking of a naked cake with fresh berries and edible flowers. Now, you tell me if you want buttercream, and I'll make it happen. Edwin has offered to play violin for the ceremony. Oh, and I just thought we could set up the reception on the beach behind Bennett's cottage, because then we can string the lights in the trees and just set the tables right up on the sand."

As Morty continued to detail his vision, Danielle actually felt a new wave of affection for her quirky, generous friend, who had just thrown himself into planning this special day without her input at all.

"Thank you, Morty."

"This means a lot to me to be able to do this for

you. You and Bennett gave me a family when my own turned their backs. This is the least I can do for you."

She hugged him tightly, realizing that his vision for a simple island wedding, surrounded by their Wisteria family, was exactly what she wanted. Maybe not some of the décor he had in mind on the Pinterest board—but still, close enough.

She just needed to convince her mother of it.

Bennett found Danielle sitting on the deck of her cottage early in the evening, staring out at the ocean with a troubled expression on her face.

"Penny for your thoughts?" he asked as he sat beside her and took her hand, admiring the engagement ring he had put on her finger.

"Just trying to figure out how exactly I'm going to tell my mother that we're *not* having a grand New York wedding without causing World War III." She showed him a series of texts from her mother, each one even more elaborate than the last.

"Ah, the formidable Cecilia Wright," he said. "You know, we could just elope."

Danielle smiled. "Don't tempt me. But no, I want

our friends here to be part of that day." She leaned her head against his shoulder. "I wish my mother understood how important this place is to us."

Bennett was quiet for a moment, thinking. "Well, what if we invited her for a visit? We can let her see the island, meet all the people we care about, and understand why we love it here so much."

She looked at him skeptically. "My mother on Wisteria Island? Oh my gosh, can you even imagine?"

"I can, actually. She might surprise you."

"Or she might try to redecorate every single cottage and organize a black-tie gala at the community center."

Bennett laughed. "Well, I'd pay good money to see that. This place could use some sprucing up. But really, Danielle, this is about more than just the wedding. You know she will be a part of our lives, and maybe it's time we build some bridges - for our future children."

She considered his words.

"Okay," she finally said. "I'll invite her to visit. But if she even *starts* measuring the community center for an art museum, I'm blaming you."

He kissed her softly. "Deal." He stood and pulled her to her feet.

"Come on. Clara is joining us for dinner over at the diner tonight. I told her about the island's music group. I think she might be interested."

"Oh, how wonderful. She needs something to spark her passion again."

They walked hand in hand toward the diner, and Bennett felt a sense of peace. Whatever challenges lay ahead for them - whether it was the wedding, planning with her mother, or helping Clara find her way through grief - they would face it all together, supported by the unlikely band of misfits they called family on Wisteria Island.

Cecilia Wright stepped off the boat onto Wisteria Island with the grace of someone accustomed to making an entrance. She wore cream linen pants and a matching jacket that remained miraculously unwrinkled despite the journey across the water. Her designer sunglasses glinted in the morning sun as she surveyed her surroundings with the critical eye that Danielle had come to know and dread.

"So this is the famous Wisteria Island," she murmured, adjusting the silk scarf around her neck.

"Mom!" Danielle called, hurrying toward her on the dock. "You made it."

Cecilia hugged her daughter, but it was obvious she was being careful not to smudge her perfectly applied lipstick. Although she was a doctor, her mother would've made an even better socialite. She loved fashion over stethoscopes, and her knowledge of the art scene in New York City couldn't be rivaled.

"Darling, of course I made it, though I must say that boat ride was quite an experience. I don't think I've been on anything smaller than a yacht since that disastrous fishing trip your father insisted we go on in '95."

Danielle laughed and linked her arm through her mother's. "Well, welcome to island life. It's a bit different from Manhattan."

"Yes, I can see that," Cecilia said, eyeing the golf cart festooned with a plastic flamingo that zipped past them. "It's charming, I suppose, in its way."

They made their way toward Danielle's cottage, and Bennett appeared, walking toward them with a warm smile.

"Dr. Wright, it's a pleasure finally meeting you in person. Welcome to Wisteria Island."

Cecilia extended her well-manicured hand. "Mr.

Alexander, I've heard so much about you, of course. Please, call me Cecilia."

"Well, only if you call me Bennett."

Cecilia studied him with the keen eye of a mother assessing her daughter's choice of life partner. Of course, Danielle knew exactly what she was thinking. Did he have a firm handshake? Did he look her directly in the eye? Was his smile genuine? Her expression softened slightly. Her mother always assessed these things in everyone she met.

"Well, Bennett, I must say your island so far is very… unique."

"That it is," he agreed, laughing. "I hope by the end of your visit, you'll see why we love it here so much."

Her eyebrow arched elegantly. "I look forward to the grand tour, but I must admit, I am having trouble envisioning a wedding here that would do justice to my daughter's standing."

Danielle shot Bennett a look that clearly said, *See what I mean?*

"Mom, why don't we get you settled in before discussing wedding stuff? Bennett had the guest cottage prepared especially for you."

"Oh, I'm not staying with you?"

"Trust me, Mom, it'll be much more comfortable

in the guest cottage, and it's near my cottage. It has a proper soaking tub and a queen-sized bed."

What Danielle really meant was that she couldn't take spending twenty-four hours a day with her often overly-critical mother. She needed evenings to recharge, so having her mother stay in the guest cottage was best for both of them.

As they continued toward the cottages, Cecilia took in every detail. Danielle saw her looking at the vibrant wisteria blooming along the pathways and then raising her hand slightly to wave at residents who waved cheerfully as they passed. She could see her mom's mind working, cataloging everything for later analysis. That's what Cecilia Wright did.

When they finally reached the guest cottage, Cecilia seemed pleasantly surprised by the tasteful decor and modern amenities.

"Oh, this is quite lovely," she finally admitted. She ran her hand over the marble countertop in the kitchenette.

"Well, I'm glad you approve," Bennett said. "I'll leave you ladies to catch up. Danielle, I've made dinner reservations at seven. Cecilia, I hope you'll join us."

"I wouldn't miss it," Cecilia said, smiling at him.

After Bennett left, she turned to her daughter. "He seems very nice."

Danielle laughed. "Well, that's high praise indeed coming from you."

It always surprised Danielle that her mother didn't automatically approve of Bennett simply because he was so wealthy. That usually was one of Cecilia's primary requirements for men that Danielle dated.

"I'm reserving final judgment," Cecilia said as she started to unpack her meticulously folded clothes. "I will say he's very handsome—nice hair, pretty eyes, and definitely smitten with you."

"Well, I'm smitten with him, too, Mom. And he's kind, generous, and treats me like an equal partner. That's more important than any good looks, money, or status."

Cecilia paused, a silk blouse in her hands. "Oh, is that a dig at me, Danielle? For wanting you to marry well?"

"Well, no, Mom, it's just…" she sighed. "It's just me trying to help you understand why I love him and why this place means so much to us." She sat on the edge of the bed. "Look, I know you want some big society wedding for me, but that's not who I am. It never has been."

Cecilia sighed and sat beside her daughter. "I just want you to have everything I didn't have, dear. Your father and I were married at the courthouse because we couldn't afford anything. I always dreamed of giving you the wedding I never had."

Danielle took her mother's hand. "I know, Mom. But you have to understand - this is *my* dream. I want to marry the man I love, surrounded by people who genuinely care about us. Not a ballroom full of social connections that I couldn't care less about."

Cecilia patted her daughter's hand. "Well, I'm here now. So show me this island of yours, and perhaps I'll begin to understand what you see here."

CHAPTER 3

Clara sat at the piano in the community center with her fingers hovering uncertainly over the keys. It had been so many months since she'd played the piano, and longer still since she felt any desire to do so. But after the enthusiastic invitation from the Wisteria Philharmonic, she was drawn here.

The small ensemble Bennett had described watched her, Janice with her violin, Frank clutching his clarinet, and Ted sitting ramrod straight beside his cello. A tiny woman named Emmy Lou sat behind a surprisingly professional-looking drum kit in the back. The people on Wisteria Island were definitely interesting characters. She'd only met a few of them in passing, but she could tell this wasn't some boring retirement community.

"We're really honored to have you join us, Mrs. Whitman," Janice said, her fun pink-tinged hair bobbing as she nodded excitedly. "We're not professionals, but we enjoy making music together. I'm also very involved in the square dancing community here, if you want to join us."

Clara thought, definitely not. Although she loved music, dancing was not her thing.

"Please call me Clara," she said, feeling oddly nervous. She'd certainly played in front of hundreds, if not thousands, of people before, but for some reason, she felt very exposed sitting in the community center of Wisteria Island.

"What piece were you all working on before I arrived?"

The four of them exchanged glances.

"Well, we were attempting *Pachelbel's Canon*," Ted said, "although we fear we weren't doing it justice. But who cares? We're just an informal little group of music lovers. We won't play in the middle of New York City or anything."

Clara nodded and smiled as she placed her hands on the keys, playing the song's opening notes. The familiar melody flowed from her fingers, muscle memory taking over, even though she'd had such a long absence from playing the piano. The others joined in, slowly, one by one, each of them hesitant at first, but then she could feel their confidence growing under her steady guidance.

It wasn't perfect—far from it. Frank came in a beat too early, and Emmy Lou's drumming was more enthusiastic than precise. This song didn't require drums, but there she was. Janice occasionally hit notes that made Clara wince internally, but there was just something undeniably joyful in their playing. They had a genuine love for music that transcended the technical limitations they obviously had.

When they reached the final measures, Clara found herself smiling. For the first time since Robert's death, a real smile reached her eyes. Music had always been their shared language, and playing it with these strangers gave her a connection to him again that felt comforting and not so painful.

"Wow, that was wonderful!" Janice exclaimed when they were finished. "You're a natural teacher, Clara."

"Well, all of you play with a ton of heart," Clara said. "And with some practice, I think we could make something special."

"So does that mean you'll come back next week?" Ted asked hopefully.

"Yes, I believe I will," Clara said.

As they packed up their instruments, they chatted about future repertoire possibilities, and Clara felt a small weight lift from her shoulders. Of course, she wasn't ready to stand up and conduct, but this small, imperfect ensemble offered something she desperately needed—a reason to engage with the world of music again, one note at a time.

M orty paced outside Dorothy's cottage, trying to gather his courage before knocking. The former movie star rarely welcomed visitors, certainly not unexpected ones, but he needed her help with the most ambitious project he'd ever taken on: Danielle and Bennett's wedding.

He took a deep breath and knocked on the door. After a long moment, it opened with a crack, revealing Dorothy's elegantly aged face.

"Morty, good lord, what on earth are you doing here at this hour?"

"It's two o'clock in the afternoon, Dorothy," he laughed. "Hardly the crack of dawn."

She waved a dismissive hand as she opened the door wider. "You know, I was in the middle of my beauty regimen. This doesn't happen by accident, you know." She gestured at her immaculately made-up face.

"And you look absolutely fabulous, darling, as always. May I come in? I have a proposition for you."

Dorothy narrowed her eyes suspiciously but opened the door and allowed him in.

"This had better be good. And if my face doesn't get moisturized properly, I'm going to look like I have elephant skin."

Morty stepped into the lavishly decorated cottage and was still impressed by Dorothy's Hollywood glamor. He'd visited her many times before, of course. They were fairly good friends, or as close of a friend as you could be to Dorothy.

She led him to a sitting area that had framed movie posters and awards from her illustrious career and pointed toward the emerald green velvet sofa that she'd kept from her home in Hollywood decades ago.

"So what's this proposition?" she asked, lighting a cigarette with a gold lighter. Morty had tried to get her to quit the habit, but she still thought it was glamorous and said she was so old now that it didn't matter what cigarettes did to her body. She felt like she had cheated fate for years.

"It's about Danielle and Bennett's wedding. I'm helping plan it, and I need someone with, well, let's just say star quality to make it truly special."

Dorothy looked interested. "Go on."

"Well, you were the queen of romantic films in your day. No one understood love and drama better than you did, and your taste is obviously impeccable." He gestured around her home. "I need your expertise to make this the most memorable wedding Wisteria Island has ever seen."

"Has Wisteria Island ever seen a wedding?"

He shrugged his shoulders. "I don't know."

"Well, flattery will get you everywhere, Morty," she said. "But why should I care about their wedding?"

Morty leaned forward. "Because Danielle is one of the few people who has never treated you like a relic or a curiosity. She sees you as a person, not just a former star. And because," he paused dramatically, "I happen to know that her mother, Cecilia Wright, is a huge fan of yours. She arrived today and will be trying to convince Danielle to have a big society wedding in New York instead of here on the island."

Dorothy's eyes widened. "Cecilia Wright. Isn't

that… isn't her mother some big doctor? Some brilliant woman?"

"Yes, she is. And she's determined to take this wedding away from us unless we can prove the island can host something so spectacular that she couldn't do the same in New York City. I mean, think of it. If they took the wedding off the island, we wouldn't be able to attend, and I know you like to attend a fancy event."

Dorothy took a long drag on her cigarette. "Well, we can't have that, can we? I mean, this island might be full of eccentrics, but this is our home. And she's part of our family. And I do owe Danielle for her discretion… regarding my medical issues."

Morty beamed. "So you'll help me?"

"I'll do more than help, darling. I'll ensure this wedding is so fabulous that even Cecilia Wright will be impressed." She stubbed out her cigarette. "Now, tell me everything you've planned so far, and then we'll figure out where you've gone wrong."

"Dr. Wright, it's Bennett Alexander. I hope I'm not disturbing you."

Bennett stood at the door of Cecilia's guest

cottage, wearing his best tailored slacks and a crisp button-down shirt, even though the island was a pretty casual atmosphere. Cecilia opened the door and looked refreshed after her journey. He figured she must have gotten a good nap.

"Not at all, Bennett. And please, I insist you call me Cecilia."

"Well, I thought you might enjoy a nice island tour before dinner, get your bearings, and maybe meet some of our residents."

"That sounds lovely," Cecilia said, slipping on a pair of comfortable walking shoes and holding her heels in her hand. "Lead the way!"

They strolled along the winding paths of Wisteria Island as Bennett pointed out different amenities - the community center with its library and game room, the small medical clinic where Danielle spent most of her days, and the charming open-air market they had just started, where residents sold homemade crafts and baked goods.

"Wow, you've really created a self-contained little world here."

"Well, that was the goal," Bennett said. "You know, a place where people can age with dignity and independence and be surrounded by friends, community, and beauty. My grandmother spent her final years in a sterile facility where she was treated mostly like a burden rather than a person who held a lifetime of wisdom and had stories to share. But I was way too young back then to do anything about it, and the first moment I had the chance, I bought this island."

Her expression softened slightly. "That's very admirable, though I must say it still is not what I envisioned for my daughter's career path. You know, Danielle was on track for a very prestigious position at Columbia Presbyterian."

He nodded, choosing his words carefully. "I know she was, and I'm sure she was exceptional at it because she's exceptional here. But on Wisteria Island, she's not just treating people's symptoms; she's caring for the whole person. She knows every single resident's medical history, yes, but she also knows their favorite books and their grandchildren's names. She knows their secret recipes." He smiled. "I believe she would tell you that she's found her calling."

Before Cecilia could respond, they were interrupted by an older man with a jaunty bow tie and a tablet tucked under his arm. He couldn't have been five feet tall.

"Bennett! There you are. I've been looking for

you. Oh my goodness, you must be Danielle's mama." He thrust out his hand enthusiastically. "I'm Morty, wedding planner extraordinaire, and the island's resident fashion guru."

Cecilia shook his hand, amused by his energy. "Cecilia Wright. Wedding planner, you say?"

"Well... self-appointed," Bennett clarified. "Morty has taken it upon himself to ensure that our wedding is 'the most spectacular event in Wisteria Island's history.'"

"Which ain't saying much, considering we've never had a wedding here before," Morty added with a wink. "But that means we've got to set the bar super high." He reached up as high as he could and barely reached the top of Bennett's head. "Dr. Wright, may I call you Cecilia? You simply *must* see my Pinterest boards. I've been gathering inspiration for weeks now."

"Weeks? They haven't been engaged that long," Cecilia said, raising an eyebrow.

"Well, I mean, we could all see where things were headed," Morty said with a knowing smile. "And now I understand you had some thoughts about a big New York shindig, but I assure you, what we're planning here will be the most magical event you've ever attended. Beach ceremony at sunset, fairy lights strung through the trees. We might even put in a dance floor right on the sand."

Bennett watched as Cecilia listened to Morty's enthusiastic description. Well, all of Morty's descriptions were enthusiastic.

"It sounds a bit unconventional," Cecilia finally said.

Morty waved his hand without missing a beat. "Well, the best things usually are. Now, if you'll excuse me, I have a meeting with Dorothy Monroe about floral arrangements. Former movie star, you know," he added in a stage whisper. "Absolutely fabulous taste."

Morty hurried off, and Cecilia turned to Bennett with a bemused expression.

"Is everyone on this island so colorful?"

Bennett said, "Yeah, pretty much. That's what makes this place special."

"And Dorothy Monroe, the movie star, lives here?"

"Yes, she does," Bennett said, shrugging his shoulders.

"Wow. Interesting. I have to say, I enjoy watching some of her old movies."

They continued their tour, passing a small beachfront area where Bennett said they hoped to hold the ceremony.

"I can see why Danielle loves it here," Cecilia said after a moment. "It is beautiful in its own way."

"She does love it, almost as much as I love her."

She studied him. "You know, Bennett, I've researched you quite thoroughly. You have very impressive business achievements, but what interests me the most is what you've done with your success. I know many rich people, and most of them don't do philanthropic things, at least not to this extent. In this case, you truly put your money where your mouth was. The island, your charitable foundation… You really seem to care about making a difference."

"I try," he said simply. "My grandmother used to say that success is measured not by what you have but by what you give to others."

"A very wise woman," Cecilia nodded. "I still have my reservations about this island wedding idea, especially if that little fella is the one that's handling everything, but I'm beginning to understand why my daughter chose you."

As they headed back toward the cottages to prepare for going out to dinner, Bennett felt a small sense of victory. Cecilia Wright was a formidable woman, no doubt about it, but she clearly wanted what was best for Danielle—and his job was to help her see that he and Wisteria Island were exactly that.

Danielle smoothed her white sundress nervously while she waited for Bennett to pick her up for dinner. So far, her mother's arrival had gone better than expected, but the evening ahead loomed with all sorts of potential pitfalls. Cecilia, in a casual island restaurant, was like setting a couture-clad cat among proverbial pigeons.

A knock at the door interrupted her thoughts.

"Ready for our big night?" Bennett asked when she opened it, looking as handsome as ever, wearing a navy blazer over a crisp white shirt.

"As I'll ever be," she said, accepting a kiss on her cheek. "How'd the tour go?"

"I think we made progress. Your mom seemed genuinely interested in the island, and of course, Morty ambushed us with wedding talk."

Danielle groaned. "Oh no, what did he say?"

"Only that he's planning the most spectacular event Wisteria Island has ever seen in its history, complete with fairy lights and a dance floor right by the ocean. Your mother was surprisingly receptive."

"Really? That doesn't sound at all like her."

"Well, let's just say not immediately dismissive might be more accurate. But let's take that as a win."

They walked to the guest cottage to pick up Cecilia, who walked out looking elegant in a simple black dress that somehow made Danielle feel under-dressed despite being in one of her nicest outfits.

"You look nice, Mom," she said.

Cecilia Wright remained strikingly beautiful at sixty-five, with her silver hair cut in a bob that framed her still-youthful face. She wondered what her mom had done at that esthetician's office, because she didn't have a wrinkle anywhere. Danielle was already starting to see the formation of crow's feet around her own eyes, so she would have to ask her mom for all the secrets as she aged.

"Thank you, darling. This island air seems to agree with me." She linked arms with her daughter as they walked toward Bennett's waiting golf cart. "Now tell me a little about this restaurant we're going to. Bennett said it's the best on the island."

"Well, it's also the *only* one on the island," Danielle admitted with a laugh. "Besides the cafeteria, which I didn't think you'd want to go to. But

Esther's cooking is genuinely excellent. She was a chef in New Orleans before she retired here."

The Wisteria Restaurant occupied a charming building overlooking the water, with its interior warm and inviting. Wooden tables, soft lighting, and large windows captured the sunset views beautifully. Several residents were already dining, and their heads turned as Danielle, Bennett, and Cecilia entered.

"Danielle! Bennett!" Esther called from behind the counter, her ample frame draped in a colorful apron. "This must be the famous Dr. Wright. Well, welcome to my humble establishment."

Cecilia smiled graciously. "Oh, do please call me Cecilia. And it's hardly humble. What a charming space you've created here."

Esther smiled at the compliment. "Your table is ready by the window, as requested, and I've prepared something special tonight. My signature seafood bouillabaisse."

As they were seated, Danielle saw several residents watching them curiously. Of course, news traveled fast around the small island, and everybody knew just how significant Cecilia's visit was.

"Your island certainly has character," Cecilia said, looking around the restaurant. "And characters," she added, nodding toward a table where Morty was deep in an animated conversation with Dorothy, who looked glamorous as always, wearing a silk scarf and oversized sunglasses, as if she was being hunted by paparazzi.

"Well, that's part of its charm," Danielle said. "Everyone here has a story, a lifetime of experiences. It makes for an interesting community."

The server brought a bottle of wine that Bennett had ordered in advance, a crisp Sancerre that Danielle knew was one of her mother's favorites.

"To family," he proposed once their glasses were filled, "and new beginnings."

They clinked glasses, and Danielle felt a moment of genuine optimism. Maybe this evening would go smoothly after all. Maybe she was overthinking everything.

"So, Cecilia," Bennett began, "Danielle tells me you're working on a new book about pandemic preparedness."

Cecilia's eyes opened wide. "Well, yes, actually. After COVID, it became clear that despite all of our advances, we remain woefully underprepared as a country when it comes to a large-scale public health emergency. My research focuses on creating more robust early warning systems and response protocols."

Cecilia launched into a passionate explanation of her work, and Danielle watched as Bennett engaged with what seemed to be genuine interest. He asked thoughtful questions and then talked about his own knowledge on the subject. Her mother was clearly impressed with him, warming to him as they talked about global health security and the challenges of coordinating international responses.

While Danielle was interested in these topics typically, all she could think about was what her mother was cooking up in that little brain of hers.

The appetizers arrived - locally caught shrimp with spicy remoulade sauce - and they momentarily paused the conversation.

"Well, this is delicious," Cecilia said. "Your chef is quite talented."

"Oh, wait until you try her main courses," Danielle said. "Esther could have had a Michelin star if she'd wanted one."

The conversation flowed as they enjoyed their meal, talking about everything from Bennett's technology ventures to Danielle's medical experiences on the island.

When the coffee and dessert arrived - a delicate

bread pudding with bourbon sauce - Cecilia steered the discussion toward wedding plans.

"While I'm beginning to see the island's appeal," she said, "I do wonder if a beach wedding is the best choice, dear. I mean, have you considered the practicalities of something like that? Weather is unpredictable, and many of your medical colleagues from New York would find attending something so far away difficult."

Danielle took a deep breath. "Mom, I appreciate your concern, but my closest friends will make the effort if it's important to me. As for my colleagues, well, my life is here now, and the people who matter most to me are currently sitting right here on this island."

"But darling, don't you want something more substantial? The Plaza has hosted the most elegant weddings in New York for generations. Your father and I always dreamed of seeing you walk down that grand staircase."

Bennett reached under the table and squeezed Danielle's hand.

"I know you did, Mom, and I'm appreciative that you want to give me everything. But this is about what *I* want and what *Bennett* wants, which is a simple, meaningful ceremony surrounded by the people who know us best and care about us. I don't care a thing in the world about a society event where half the guests are just there for appearances."

Her mom looked momentarily hurt. "Well, I suppose I've been planning your wedding in my head since you were a little girl. Sometimes it's hard to let go of those visions."

"I understand that," Danielle said gently. "And I want you to be involved. But it needs to be our wedding, not yours. You already had your chance."

After a moment, Cecilia nodded. "Well, perhaps I should at least see what your friend Morty has in mind before I make any judgments. I mean, his enthusiasm is definitely infectious."

Danielle exchanged a glance with Bennett. "So, really? You'd be open to his ideas?"

"Well, I didn't say *that*. I said I'd look at them. There's a difference."

Bennett chuckled. "I think that's fair. And I should say, for Morty's ideas, we need to warn you that he's now recruited Dorothy to help with the planning, which means everything is likely to be over the top. She's quite a presence on the island, but she always keeps to herself."

As they finished their dessert, Danielle felt a tiny sliver of optimism. Her mother hadn't exactly embraced the idea of an island wedding, but she wasn't actively fighting it anymore, either. It was progress, however small.

The evening concluded, and they walked back to the cottages under a canopy of stars. Danielle felt Bennett's arm slip around her waist.

"That went pretty well," he murmured.

"Better than I expected," she said. "I'm not sure how I feel about my mother and Morty joining forces to plan my wedding."

"It *is* a terrifying prospect," Bennett said. "But at least they'll be working toward the same goal—making our day special."

At the guest cottage, Cecilia kissed her daughter's cheek.

"Thank you for a lovely evening, dear. I'll see you in the morning. Perhaps you could show me your clinic tomorrow. I'd like to see your setup here."

"I'd like that," Danielle said.

Cecilia disappeared into the cottage, and Bennett pulled Danielle close.

"See? Progress."

"Baby steps," Danielle said. "Tiny little baby steps."

CHAPTER 4

Clara sat on her porch in the morning, sipping tea and watching the island come to life. After her music session recently, she'd slept so much better than she had in months. Although the familiar ache of grief was still ever-present, it just felt a little bit less overwhelming. She felt a little bit less alone.

A movement caught her eye. A tall, elegant woman was walking along the path. She wasn't one of the regular residents. She definitely didn't look like she belonged here. But something about her reminded Clara of symphony board members she'd dealt with throughout her career—confident, sophisticated, and used to being in charge.

The woman walked closer and noticed Clara. She paused.

"Good morning," she called. "I don't think we've met. I'm Cecilia Wright, Danielle's mother."

Clara set down her teacup. "Clara Whitman. I'm actually new to the island."

"Do you mind if I join you? I'm just taking my morning walk, trying to get acquainted with the place."

"Oh, please," Clara said, gesturing to the empty chair beside her.

Cecilia settled gracefully onto the porch and looked around the cottage.

"So you've recently arrived as well? What brings you to this unique community?"

There was something in her tone that suggested she was trying to understand the appeal of the island, and Clara found herself unexpectedly defensive about her new home.

"I lost my husband six months ago," she said. "We spent decades traveling the world for our careers, and I felt like I needed somewhere quiet to recalibrate."

"I'm sorry for your loss. Losing a spouse changes everything, I would assume. Especially after a long marriage."

Clara nodded. "It does. Suddenly, your future

plans vanish, and you're left wondering what comes next."

"What was your career, if you don't mind me asking?"

"I was in an orchestra. I was also a conductor for twenty years. My husband as well."

Cecilia's eyes showed genuine interest. "Oh, how fascinating. I've always envied people who have musical talent. My research work keeps me firmly in the realm of science and data."

"Research?"

"Epidemiology. I specialize in infectious disease control and pandemic preparedness."

"Oh, wow, that sounds very important."

"It is," Cecilia said. "Although sometimes I wonder if I focus too much on my career at the expense of other things that are more important in life." She looked down the road toward Danielle's cottage. "Children grow up so quickly, and then suddenly they're making all kinds of life decisions you never anticipated."

Clara smiled. "So you're here about Danielle's wedding plans?"

"Well, I'm trying to provide guidance, yes. Though I'm discovering that my daughter and her soon-to-be husband have definite ideas of their own."

"Well, that's not surprising. They both strike me as people who know their own minds."

"Well, Danielle always has," Cecilia said with a slight smile. "Even as a child, she was determined to chart her own course. I wanted her to be a research physician just like me, but she insisted on hands-on patient care."

They sat in silence for a moment.

"You know, Bennett seems very devoted to this place and to Danielle. They both have been so very kind to me," Clara said. "When I arrived here, I was in a dark place, and they've really gone out of their way to make me feel welcome."

"Well, I suppose that's what matters the most, isn't it? Finding people who truly care."

Before Clara could say anything else, they were interrupted by the arrival of Morty, who ran up the path with his usual enthusiasm.

"Clara, good morning! Oh, Dr. Wright, what a pleasant surprise." He smiled at both of them. "I was coming to invite Clara to our planning meeting this afternoon. Dorothy and I are discussing wedding flowers, and Clara agreed to help us with the music, so I thought she should be involved."

"Wedding flowers?" Cecilia said, raising an eyebrow.

"Oh yes. We're thinking wisteria, of course, but we also need other flowers. Maybe some white roses or some sea lavender for a coastal touch. Dorothy insists that we need something dramatic for the ceremony arch, but I think she's thinking about cascading orchids to make it very cinematic."

Clara watched Cecilia's expression.

"Orchids would be lovely," Cecilia said, "though they are notoriously difficult to keep fresh in an outdoor setting."

"You know about flowers?" Morty said, his eyes widening.

"I chaired the New York Botanical Garden Benefit for five years. One picks up a few things," Cecilia said.

"Well, then you simply must join us! Dorothy would be thrilled to meet you, and we could use your expertise. How about three o'clock at the community center?"

Cecilia hesitated for a moment, then nodded. "Well, I suppose I could stop by. It's not like I have a whole lot else to do on this island. I'd be there purely in an advisory capacity, of course."

"Of course," Morty agreed. "Clara, can you come too?"

Clara nodded, seeming to get caught up in Morty's infectious enthusiasm. "I'll be there."

As Morty hurried off to spread the news, Cecilia turned to Clara.

"Is he always so exuberant?"

Clara offered, "I mean, from what I've seen so far, yes. There's something very refreshing about his enthusiasm, especially on an island full of retired people."

"Indeed," Cecilia said, standing up from her chair. "Well, I suppose I should continue my exploration of Wisteria Island. It was lovely meeting you, Clara, and maybe I'll see you at the planning session later."

Bennett sat at his desk reviewing quarterly financial reports. Even though he lived in an idyllic island setting, maintaining this community of older people required very careful financial management. Between the health care costs, infrastructure maintenance, and salaries for the staff, the expenses were substantial. And although his technology investments continued to perform well, it was all on him to provide the necessary funding.

A knock at his office door interrupted his concentration.

"Come in," he called. As he looked up, he found Naomi, his assistant, standing there with a concerned expression and her hands on her hips.

"Sorry to bother you, but there's quite a situation at the community center that might need your attention."

Bennett sighed, pushing his papers aside. "What kind of situation?"

"Well, Morty and Dorothy have taken over the main room for wedding planning, which was fine at first, but now Dr. Wright has joined them, and let's just say things are getting a bit heated."

"Heated how?"

Naomi winced. "I think there's some kind of disagreement about color schemes and flower arrangements, and maybe the entire concept of even having a beach wedding. I heard the phrase 'sand in Louboutins' mentioned several times."

Bennett rubbed his temples. "And where's Danielle?"

"She's at the clinic with Mamie. She's had another episode with her blood pressure."

"Of course," Bennett said. "I'll handle it."

He made his way to the community center and mentally prepared for diplomatic negotiations with Danielle's mother. Cecilia was a formidable opponent, but he suspected she wasn't entirely against the island wedding. She just wanted to make sure it was an elegant affair.

The scene that greeted him was even more chaotic than he'd anticipated. The large table in the center of the room was covered in flower catalogs, fabric swatches, and what looked like architectural sketches of some sort of elaborate structure. Morty and Dorothy stood to one side, gesturing animatedly, while Cecilia stood there, clearly composed but firm on the other side. Clara sat slightly apart, looking slightly amused but more overwhelmed than anything. This was not a good first impression of the island when it came to Clara.

"A tent is simply not sufficient protection against the elements," Cecilia said, "and if you insist on an outdoor ceremony, we need a proper pavilion with a solid roof."

"The tent has a romantic, ethereal quality," Morty argued, as he held his hands in the air like he was catching butterflies or something, "all billowing in the breeze like something out of a fairy tale."

"Until that breeze becomes a sandstorm and then the whole thing collapses on the bride, who happens to be my daughter," Cecilia said, putting her hand on her hip.

Dorothy looked glamorous as always, wearing her silk caftan and oversized sunglasses indoors for reasons Bennett would never understand. She nodded.

"Cecilia has a point, darling. I remember when I filmed *Summer Storms* in '62. An unexpected squall destroyed the entire set. Ruined three Dior gowns and gave poor Rock Hudson a concussion when a palm tree fell on him."

Bennett cleared his throat, drawing all of their attention. "I see wedding planning is well underway."

"Bennett!" Morty exclaimed. "Thank goodness you're here. Perhaps you can help us resolve some creative differences."

"I don't think I'm the one you want weighing in on design decisions," Bennett said, "but I *am* interested in what it is you're all planning."

Cecilia set her gaze on him. "I was trying to explain the practical considerations of an outdoor wedding. I know it sounds really romantic to have a beach ceremony, but there are significant logistical challenges."

"Which we're prepared to address," Bennett said. "What specific concerns do you have?"

"Weather contingencies, for one," Cecilia replied. "Guest comfort, for another. And honestly, the level of sophistication is just not possible in such a setting."

"All valid points. But what if we could combine the natural beauty of the island with the elegance and security you're concerned about?"

"I'm listening," Cecilia said, crossing her arms.

Bennett moved to the table and picked up a pencil, turning over one of the sketches to its blank side. "What if, instead of a temporary structure, we built something permanent? A gazebo overlooking the water that's designed specifically for a wedding, but then will remain as an amenity for the island afterward."

He started simple sketching as he spoke, showing an elegant structure with open sides that could be enclosed with panels if there was inclement weather.

"So we could incorporate the elements of both visions: that open, airy feeling as long as weather allows, with the security and elegance you're concerned about."

Dorothy leaned forward. "You know, with the right lighting, that could be quite dramatic. Maybe we could wrap the columns with wisteria and fairy lights."

"Well, it would need a proper floor," Cecilia added, "so no one has to navigate sand in formal shoes."

"Of course," Bennett agreed. "We could even position it so the ocean will form a natural backdrop for the ceremony."

Clara, who had been mostly quiet until now, spoke up. "From a musical perspective, a structure would also provide better acoustics than an open beach. The sound won't dissipate as quickly."

Morty clapped his hands excitedly. "Oh my gosh, I love it! The best of both worlds. I love it when a plan comes together. And then we would have a lasting reminder of their special day!"

Bennett watched as Cecilia studied his rough sketch.

"You know... it has potential," she finally admitted. "Though the devil is in the details, Bennett. Materials, design, timeline..."

"All things we can work out," Bennett reassured her. "The important thing is that we find a solution that honors what Danielle wants, while also addressing your very practical concerns."

"You're quite the diplomat, aren't you?"

"I try," he said, "especially when it comes to matters close to my heart."

The tension in the room had finally dissipated, and everyone started discussing possibilities for the gazebo. Bennett stepped back and allowed them to work, pleased that Cecilia was actively engaging with Morty and Dorothy rather than dismissing their ideas.

Clara moved to stand beside him.

"Very nicely handled," she said quietly. "You found a way to make everybody feel heard."

"It's what I do," Bennett said, shrugging his shoulders. "I try to build bridges, literal and figurative."

"And Danielle is very lucky to have you," Clara said softly. "Robert was like that too, always finding harmony in the discord."

"Thank you. That means a lot," Bennett said.

He watched as the planning session continued with renewed enthusiasm, and then slipped out to find Danielle. She should be the one making these decisions, after all. The wedding was mostly for her. He hoped the gazebo sounded like a good idea to her, too, since it had been a spontaneous suggestion. But the more he thought about it, the more it felt right to have the ocean as the backdrop to their special day.

Danielle hurried toward the community center with her medical bag slung over her shoulder. She had just received Bennett's cryptic text that said, *Come quick. Wedding summit in progress,* while she finished Mamie's blood pressure check.

I mean, what could possibly constitute a "wedding summit" that required her immediate attention? The thought of it filled her with equal parts dread and curiosity.

She approached the building and heard raised voices through the open windows. She could pick out her mother's crisp, authoritative tone flying through the air, just like it was yesterday, and she was a young child listening to her mother harp on her about grades. It contrasted with Morty's theatrical exclamations and the smoky drawl of Dorothy's voice. She also heard Bennett occasionally try to cut through with the voice of reason, but he wasn't getting a word in edgewise.

Pausing in the doorway, she took in the scene. Fabric swatches scattered across tables. Flower catalogs splayed open. Sketches pinned on a makeshift display board. Her mother, Morty, and Dorothy were clustered around Bennett, who was trying to draw something on a piece of paper, while Clara watched nearby. None of them had noticed her yet, which gave her a minute to observe what was going on.

"The columns need to be substantial," her mother said, gesturing with her elegant, manicured hands. "We don't want anything rustic or flimsy. We want timeless elegance, not some beach shack."

"We don't want it to look like a Greek temple either," Morty said. "It needs to be whimsical, romantic."

"What it needs," Dorothy interjected, finally removing her sunglasses for emphasis, "is dramatic sightlines. Every good director knows that framing is everything. When Danielle makes her grand entrance, all eyes should be drawn to her."

Bennett nodded. "Okay, well, what if we position it here, on the slight rise overlooking the cove? And then the ocean will form a natural backdrop—but we're elevated enough to avoid any issues with the tides or wet sand."

"Well, that's actually quite perfect," Cecilia said. "And the structure itself?"

"An octagonal gazebo," Bennett said. "Classic design, but, you know, clean modern lines. Large enough to accommodate the wedding party itself, and intimate enough to feel connected to the guests sitting on the lawn."

Danielle felt her heart skip a beat. A gazebo on her favorite spot overlooking the cove. She could just picture it—standing there with Bennett as the sun set over the water, surrounded by all the people they loved.

"I love it," she said, finally stepping into the room. Everyone turned her way.

"Danielle, darling!" Morty exclaimed. "We were just brainstorming some ideas for your beautiful wedding."

"I see that," she said, looking at Bennett's sketch. It was rough, and he was definitely not an artist, but it showed a beautiful octagonal structure with an elegant domed roof and had the most picturesque view behind it.

"It's not just for the wedding," Bennett explained. "I thought maybe we could build something permanent that everyone could enjoy for years to come."

"That could be quite an undertaking," Danielle said. "I mean, the construction, the cost…"

"Worth every penny," he said, taking her hand. "And perfect timing. I've been wanting to add some gathering space for residents—you know, something for sunrise yoga or sunset concerts."

Cecilia cleared her throat. "I must say the concept has potential. With the right materials and design, it could look quite sophisticated."

"Wait, so you *like* the idea of an island wedding now?"

Cecilia looked at her daughter. "I told you I'd keep an open mind. And the gazebo concept is something that could address a lot of practical concerns, but honor your wish for a natural setting."

"Translation: your mother's brilliant design suggestions have elevated our humble beach wedding to something worthy of *Architectural Digest*," Morty whispered, earning a glare and half-smile from Cecilia.

Danielle walked closer and examined some of the materials and drawings. "So y'all have all been planning this without me? Together?"

"Well, we were going to present it to you when we had a concrete proposal," Bennett said, apologizing. "I mean, it just sort of evolved this afternoon."

"It started as a tent discussion and escalated a little bit quicker than we anticipated," Clara added with a small smile. "Although your mother makes very compelling arguments about weather problems."

Danielle couldn't help but laugh. "Oh, I'm sure she does."

She studied the sketch carefully and tried to imagine what the gazebo would look like on her wedding day. The idea of creating something that would last and remain part of Wisteria Island long after their wedding day felt good to her.

"So when could we start building?"

"Well, as soon as we finalize the design. I have contractors who work with us regularly. I'm sure they could begin soon."

"You think so? So quickly?"

Cecilia looked surprised.

"Yeah, that's one of the advantages of being the island's owner. I can expedite certain projects when motivated," Bennett said, smiling.

Dorothy clapped her hands decisively. "Well, then it's settled. A gazebo it shall be. And we can now move on to the important matters like the color scheme. I'm thinking sea glass tones. You know, greens, soft blues, maybe a touch of frosted white."

"With just a hint of blush," Morty added, "for romance."

As Dorothy and Morty launched into an

animated discussion about fabric, Bennett pulled Danielle aside quietly.

"Are you really okay with all of this?" he asked. "It all happened so quickly, and I don't want you to feel steamrolled."

Danielle squeezed his hand. "It's perfect, Bennett. Truly. I adore the idea of creating something that will last beyond our wedding day."

"And your mom seems to be coming around," he said, as he looked over at Cecilia, who was showing Clara some different flower arrangements she found in a magazine. "I'm actually in shock. I expected her to fight the island wedding idea tooth and nail."

"You must be magic. What did you say to her?"

"Nothing special," he said, shrugging. "I think she's just seeing how the community cares about us, and it's making an impression. She has excellent taste. And once she realized that she could contribute something, she became more invested."

Danielle watched her mother speaking with Clara in such an animated way that she was surprised. It was a side of her mom she rarely saw, that creative, passionate woman beneath the cool, professional exterior she showed everyone.

"I think I might need to rescue Clara," Danielle

said with a small smile. "My mom can be quite over-whelming when she gets excited about a project."

She moved to join the others and felt a wave of gratitude wash over her. Just a few days ago, she'd been dreading her mother coming to visit Wisteria Island. She believed there would be an inevitable conflict about wedding plans, but now Cecilia Wright was actually working with Morty and Dorothy on gazebo designs and color schemes.

Life was funny. Wisteria Island continued to always work its special magic on people, bringing together the most unlikely folks and creating connections where none seemed possible before.

"So, Mom," Danielle said, walking over to the group, "tell me about this gazebo vision of yours."

"Well, darling, I'm thinking classic white columns with just a touch of maybe some decorative lattice-work. I'm not a big fan of lattice normally, but I could see it here. Nothing too ornate, of course, but we want to make it a focal point. The roof, of course, should have a graceful curve. And the perfect dome would be too formal, but maybe a slight pitch would look unfinished."

She put her index finger on her chin as she looked up at the ceiling and thought about her plans.

Danielle caught Bennett's eye from across the room. He winked at her before slipping out the door.

The gazebo, this permanent structure overlooking the beautiful ocean, would be more than a wedding venue. It would be a symbol of their life together. Built on a solid foundation, but open to the beauty around them and designed to weather any storms that might come their way.

CHAPTER 5

Clara sat at her beloved piano on Saturday morning with her fingers hovering hesitantly over the keys. After yesterday's wedding planning session, she'd gone home with an unfamiliar energy she hadn't felt in months. There was a restlessness that couldn't be satisfied by her normal quiet reading or staring out at the ocean. It was almost as if her creativity was starting to fight with her grief.

For the first time since her husband's death, she felt an urge to play the piano, not just to accompany the island's ensemble, but to really play the way she used to when music was just as essential to her as breathing.

She put her hands on the keys and started to tentatively play a simple Bach prelude, one of the first pieces she had mastered as a small child. The notes came back to her with muscle memory, just like riding a bike, as her fingers remembered what her heart had tried to forget. The melody filled the cottage, and she closed her eyes, allowing the music to wash over her.

Yes, every note hurt—a reminder of Robert, of their shared passion, of all she'd lost. But there was something else there too, something she hadn't expected at all.

Comfort.

It was like finding an old friend waiting patiently for her to return.

She transitioned into a Chopin nocturne as her confidence grew with each note. This one had been one of Robert's favorites. It was timeless. He would often sit beside her on the bench as she played, with his eyes closed, occasionally humming softly to the melody. A tear slipped down her cheek, but she didn't stop playing.

For so long, she had avoided anything that reminded her too much of her beloved husband. The grief would just consume her, she feared. But now her fingers danced across the keys like they always had, and she realized that music wasn't a reminder of her loss. It was her connection to him, a way to keep him close to her.

The final notes of the song lingered in the air, and she sat motionless with her hands resting lightly on the keys. The silence that followed felt different from the grief-stricken, empty silence of recent months.

It felt full of possibility.

A knock at her door startled her. Wiping away a stray tear, she stood to answer it and found Danielle on her porch with a small white wicker basket.

"Good morning. I brought you some muffins from the bakery," Danielle said, smiling. Then her expression shifted to concern. "Oh no, Clara, are you okay? Have you been crying?"

Clara touched her own cheek. "Oh, I'm just a bit emotional this morning. I played piano for the first time since… well, in a long time."

"I thought I heard music as I walked up," Danielle said gently. "It was lovely."

"Thank you. Please do come in." Clara stepped aside, aware that dust had accumulated on various surfaces. She hadn't been particularly diligent about her house cleaning since arriving on the island. But Danielle didn't seem to notice or care, and put the basket on the kitchen counter.

"Maxine's blueberry muffins are absolutely legendary around here. I just thought you might enjoy some. I hope you like them."

"That's very kind," Clara said. "Would you like some tea? I was just about to make a pot."

Danielle nodded, and Clara busied herself in the kitchen with the kettle. She saw Danielle wander over to the piano.

"You play beautifully," she said. "I love watching people play piano. The way their hands move over the keys is like watching a dance. I was never particularly gifted with musical talents."

Clara smiled. "Music has always been my language. I think I express myself better through playing than words."

"I get that. For me, it's taking care of people. Sometimes a simple act of care communicates more than anything else I could say."

Danielle accepted the cup of tea that Clara offered. Clara loved to use her mother's teacups. She'd broken several over the years, but she still had three that she cherished, almost as much as anything else she owned. They were white bone china, very delicate, with pink roses on them.

"How did you find yesterday's wedding planning

session? I hope my mother wasn't too over-whelming."

Clara laughed. "You know, it was very entertaining. Your mother is, let's say, formidable, but in a very impressive way. And she clearly loves you."

"She does," Danielle said. "Although we often have very different ideas about what's best for me. I was actually surprised to see her so agreeable about the gazebo."

"I think she just appreciated being included," Clara said, sitting down across from Danielle at the small kitchen table, "and having her expertise valued. You know, sometimes as we get older, we start to feel irrelevant. I'm sure your mother doesn't struggle with that, at least not right now. She's still in the working world and very well thought of. But sometimes, just having other people take your opinion into consideration is all an older person wants. Sometimes we feel like our wisdom means nothing, and that people don't want to hear from us anymore."

"I hope you don't feel that way here," Danielle said. "We're all one big family, although we don't always get along. But I know your input here is already very valuable to everyone who's met you."

"Thank you," Clara said.

"And you're probably right about my mom. I had been so focused on asserting my independence with her that I might have excluded her unnecessarily."

They sat for a moment, sipping their tea without any words.

"You know, I've been thinking," Clara said finally, "about the music for your wedding. If you'd like, I could play the piano at the ceremony. If you don't want piano, I totally understand. But I could help coordinate the other musicians as well."

Danielle's face lit up. "Really? Clara, that would be wonderful. I would be so honored."

"Oh, it would give me a purpose," Clara said. "You know, something to focus on besides all the grief. To be honest, after yesterday, I'm feeling a little more connected to things, to people."

"Well, I'm so glad to hear that. I've found the island has a way of healing people. Not by making pain go away or erasing memories, but by surrounding you with other people who've been through it and understand it. And they help you carry it."

"You know, Robert would have loved it here," she said softly. "He always said music was about connection. The connection between notes, between musicians, between the performer and the audience. I really think he would appreciate how this community connects with each other."

"Tell me about him," Danielle said. "What was he like as a conductor?"

Her eyes crinkled as she smiled, remembering him. "Oh, magnetic. When Robert stepped onto the podium, everyone, musicians and audience alike, felt it. It was energizing, like electricity was in the air. He had a head full of unruly white hair that made him kind of look like that crazy doctor on *Back to the Future,* and he had this amazing ability to draw performances out of musicians that they didn't even know they were capable of. He never intimidated, like some conductors do. He inspired them."

She shared stories about her husband. About his passionate interpretation of Brahms, his infamous battles with opera divas, and his ritual of eating exactly three almond cookies before every performance.

She could feel the knot of grief in her chest loosen slightly. It didn't disappear. She didn't imagine it ever would. But it was transforming into something that could coexist with warmth, and even occasional laughter.

"Well, he sounds like a remarkable man," Danielle said. "Thank you for sharing him with me."

Clara was surprised to realize they'd been talking for nearly an hour, and the tea had long since gone cold in her cup.

"I'm so sorry I've been rambling on."

"Not at all," Danielle said. "I loved hearing about him. And I'm honored that you want to play at our wedding."

"It feels right," Clara said. "Not only is it a way to honor Robert's memory, but it's also a way to usher in a new love story and a new life together with you and Bennett."

Danielle paused at the door before getting ready to leave for her morning clinic hours.

"You know, there's a small concert in the community center this evening, just some residents sharing their talents. Maybe you could go and listen to them? See if any of them would be good for our wedding?"

Clara nodded. "I think I'd like that."

After Danielle left, Clara returned to the piano, her fingers finding the keys with renewed purpose. This time she played one of Robert's compositions, a piece he'd written for their 25th anniversary. As music filled the cottage, she felt something shift. The pain of loss was still there, a constant companion. But now something was there alongside of it - hope.

Bennett stood on the grassy bluff overlooking the cove and tried to imagine the gazebo that would soon stand in that spot. The gentle breeze carried with it the scent of saltwater and blooming wisteria.

"So this is the spot?" Eddie asked, standing beside him with a clipboard and measuring tape.

"This is it," Bennett said. "Perfect vantage point. Ocean views, elevated enough to not worry about any concerns with the tides."

Eddie nodded, making notes and grunting. "We'll need to pour concrete footings and ensure it's stable. That means digging down pretty deep."

"Whatever it takes," Bennett said. "This needs to be built to last."

"Like your relationship with Danielle," Eddie grinned, his weathered face crinkling at the corners.

Bennett laughed. "Well, that was very poetic, Eddie, but exactly like that."

He had called Eddie at dawn, eager to get the project moving along. The island's maintenance supervisor had been with Bennett since the very beginning, helping to transform an overgrown patch of coastal land into a vibrant community.

"The builders can start Monday," Eddie said, pacing off the dimensions. "I've already called Miguel's team on the mainland. They said they'd clear their schedule because they owe you for getting Miguel's mother into that specialist in Atlanta last year."

"They don't owe me anything," Bennett said. "It was just the right thing to do, but I'm glad they can fit us in quickly."

Eddie snorted. "Yeah, well, not everybody does the right thing these days. Anyhow, they're excited to get started, so they'll make it their best work yet."

Bennett nodded. Miguel's construction company had built several structures on the island and always had exceptional craftsmanship. They understood the coastal environment and how to create buildings that could take the salt air and occasional storms.

"I've got Cecilia's drawings here," Eddie said, pulling out several sheets of paper. "Woman knows what she wants, I'll give her that. She was very specific about the column design."

"She has excellent taste," Bennett said, "and a keen eye for detail. I drew the first pictures, but she took them away from me and made something much better looking."

"Like mother, like daughter with the keen eye for

detail," Eddie said. "Danielle nearly drove me crazy with her requests when we were rebuilding her cottage after the hurricane. 'Two inches to the left, Eddie.' 'Can we raise this window six inches, Eddie?' But, you know, she was right about it every time."

Bennett laughed, remembering how particular Danielle had been about her new home. Her attention to detail and insistence on getting things right were among the many things he loved about her.

"Speaking of Danielle," Eddie said, "does she know you're out here at the crack of dawn getting this started?"

"Not exactly. I wanted to surprise her with how quickly we can make progress. So, the gazebo was decided yesterday. I'm hoping we can have it substantially complete within a couple of weeks."

Eddie whistled. "Wow, that's ambition. Ambitious even from Miguel's team."

"I know. But we've got resources, and I'm willing to pay whatever it takes to get this thing going." He looked out over the water. "I want Danielle to be able to see it, to walk through it, and really visualize our wedding day, not just look at sketches."

Eddie nodded. "You're a good man, Bennett. Danielle's lucky to have found you."

"Oh, I'm the lucky one," Bennett replied softly.

They spent the next hour taking measurements and discussing all the technical details—the depth of the foundation, the materials for the columns, the design of the roof. Bennett wanted everything to be perfect.

As they worked, several residents strolled by on their morning walks, curious about what was going on. News of the gazebo and its purpose as Danielle and Bennett's wedding venue had spread quickly through the island's very efficient grapevine.

"Morning, fellas," Gladys called, approaching with her tiny dog trotting beside her. "Marking out for the wedding spot, are you?"

"That's right," Bennett said. "The gazebo will stand right here."

Gladys smiled, her weathered face crinkling. "Well, how wonderful. You know, Harold proposed to me in a gazebo. We were in Savannah in 1962. He was so nervous that he dropped the ring. We had to get down on our hands and knees and find it in the cracks between the floorboards."

Bennett smiled. "Well, we'll make sure the floorboards are nice and tight."

"See that you do," she said with a wink. "Oh, and make sure it's big enough for me to get up there and dance afterward. These old bones still remember how to cut a rug, you know."

As Gladys continued on her way, Eddie laughed. "I think this whole island is invested in this wedding now."

"Well, it's their celebration too, in a way," Bennett said. "These people are our family."

By mid-morning, they had completed the preliminary measurements and marked the foundation outline with bright orange spray paint. Eddie headed off to call the contractors and left Bennett alone on the bluff.

He stood in the center of what would become the gazebo, turning slowly to take in the view from all angles. This is where he would meet Danielle—his wife—and they would begin the next chapter of their lives together. The thought filled him with such a profound sense of rightness.

His phone buzzed with a text from Danielle.

> Where are you? Morty's looking everywhere, says he has urgent questions about wedding cake flavors.

Bennett smiled and typed back.

> At the future gazebo site with Eddie, taking measurements for builders. Hide while you still can.

Her reply came a few seconds later.

> Too late. He found me. We are debating the merits of lemon curd versus raspberry filling. Send help.

Laughing, Bennett put his phone back in his pocket and took one last look at the marked-out gazebo footprint before heading toward the center of the island.

As he walked, he calculated timelines and logistics, determined to create something truly special for his future wife.

The gazebo would be more than just a wedding venue. It would be his gift to her, to the island, and to their future together. And one day, he hoped to be sitting in that gazebo with their children—a place where they would make memories for years to come.

Morty paced back and forth with anxious energy as he crossed Dorothy's living room. He kept checking his watch and felt like he had done it three times in the last two minutes.

"Oh, she's late," he fretted. "What if she's changed her mind? What if she has decided to whisk Danielle away back to New York City for some big society wedding after all?"

Dorothy, elegantly arranged in her purple velvet chaise lounge, didn't look up from her magazine.

"Oh, dear Morty, she'll be here. Cecilia Wright is a woman who keeps her appointments. Plus, I don't think she's the type to kidnap her own daughter."

"But it's already ten past three. The florist's samples will be wilting."

"Calm yourself, darling. A proper entrance is always a little fashionably late." She turned a page slowly in her magazine. "Besides, anticipation heightens the impact."

Morty wasn't convinced, but before he could say anything else, a crisp knock sounded at the door. He practically leapt to answer it.

Cecilia was standing on the porch, looking immaculate in cream linen pants and a coral-colored blouse.

"Dr. Wright, we were just—"

"Cecilia, please," she said, holding up her hand. "And I'm sorry for my tardiness. I was on a call with my publisher that ran longer than expected."

"Not at all, you're right on time," Dorothy called from the chaise, taking a sip of her mimosa. "Morty simply arrived obscenely early, as is his habit."

Cecilia crossed to Dorothy and extended her hand. "I wanted to properly introduce myself and tell you that I've admired your work for many years."

Dorothy accepted the handshake. "The admiration is mutual. I've actually read some of your research papers."

"You've read my research?" Cecilia said, pleasantly surprised.

"Oh, I make it a point to stay informed. Just because I played vapid socialites on screen doesn't mean I actually am one. Although I *am* wearing a muumuu and drinking a mimosa in my velvet chaise," she said, smiling slightly.

"Well, I would never assume you were one. In fact, I've always thought of your performances as showing remarkable intelligence beneath all that glamor."

Morty watched the two formidable women size each other up. It was like watching two regal cats decide whether to share the same territory.

"Now then," Cecilia said, "I understand we're finalizing floral arrangements today."

"Yes," Morty said, clapping. He was happy to return to the agenda. He ran to the dining table where he had laid out various sample arrangements, color swatches, and more sketches.

"Now, the florist sent these for our approval. I am leaning toward the white roses with sea lavender and a touch of wisteria, of course."

Cecilia looked at the samples with a critical eye. "The palette is pretty, but I'm concerned about the structure of this arrangement. For the gazebo columns, we need something more vertically dramatic."

"That's exactly what I said," Dorothy said as she slowly stood up and joined them at the table. "The columns need a cascading element, something that will draw the eye upward."

"Well, maybe orchids," Cecilia said, "but integrated with trailing jasmine or clematis for movement."

Morty watched them in fascination as they started rearranging all the elements, their heads bent together over the samples. Even though they came from very different backgrounds, they shared an impressive innate sense of aesthetics.

"The gazebo is going to be white, correct?" Cecilia said, making notes in a small leather-bound notebook.

"Yes, with subtle gray undertones so that it won't look so stark against the natural setting," Morty said.

"Well, then we need warmth in the flowers to soften the overall effect. Blush pink, perhaps, with maybe some pale peach." Cecilia selected several color swatches and arranged them in a fan-like shape. "Something like this."

Dorothy nodded. "Oh yes, that will photograph beautifully against the ocean backdrop. But we must think about the light. A late afternoon wedding will have a golden quality that will enhance these tones."

For the next hour, the three of them worked through every single detail of floral design—from the gazebo decorations to the bridal bouquet, from boutonnieres to centerpieces.

Morty was amazed how Cecilia just folded right into their planning process.

"You have quite the eye for design," he said as Cecilia sketched an arrangement for the gazebo entrance.

"Well, I've chaired my share of fundraisers and galas. One develops a certain sense for these things."

"It's more than that," Dorothy observed. "You

have a natural talent. I think in another life, you could have been a designer yourself. Do you believe in reincarnation?"

Cecilia chuckled. "Not really. I am a scientist, after all. But perhaps I could have been a designer. My mother was an artist, actually. But science was always my calling."

"So is it difficult balancing a demanding career with family life?" Morty asked.

Cecilia was quiet for a moment. "Oh yes. I was often absent when Danielle was growing up. Her father was a doctor too. We had conferences and research trips. I spent endless hours in the lab."

"But you clearly adore her," Morty said.

"Oh, more than anything. However, I haven't always been good at showing it. I wanted her to have every opportunity and every advantage. Sometimes I pushed too hard and tried to shape her path instead of letting her find her own way."

Dorothy nodded. "It's the eternal maternal dilemma. Mothers want to protect them from their mistakes and only find out that they're making new ones."

"Oh, do you have children, Ms. Monroe?"

A shadow passed over Dorothy's face. "No. I always wanted children, but it was never meant to be for me, I suppose. I spent a lot of time away from home on movie sets, so I guess it was for the best at the time. It's quite lonely now, not having any family to visit me, though."

Morty knew Dorothy's painful history and reached out to squeeze her hand supportively.

Cecilia broke her silence. "You know, that's why this wedding is so important to me. This is my chance to show Danielle that I care about her and support her in a way I often didn't show. To show her that I support her choices, even when they're different from what I might have chosen."

"Then we shall make it perfect," Dorothy said, putting her hand on Cecilia's shoulder. "A celebration worthy of the love that Bennett and Danielle have found with each other."

Morty felt his eyes welling with tears, as they often did.

"Tissues, Morty," Dorothy offered, rolling her eyes.

"I'm fine, I'm fine," he said, dabbing at his eyes with the back of his hand. "Just a bit of pollen from all these flowers."

Cecilia chuckled. "You care deeply for them, too, don't you? Danielle and Bennett?"

"Oh, they're family. The first real family I've had in a long time," Morty said.

"Now, shall we discuss table linens?" Cecilia said, changing the subject. "I have some thoughts about incorporating a tiny, subtle pattern that complements all the floral design."

As they returned to wedding planning, Morty felt a sense of connection with Cecilia Wright, something he had never expected. Through her polished exterior was a woman trying to bridge the gap with her daughter. And if their little island wedding could help heal that relationship—well, then that would be the most beautiful decoration of all.

CHAPTER 6

The community center hummed with activity as the residents gathered for a talent showcase. Clara stood at the entrance, hesitating, suddenly very uncertain about attending. She had told Danielle that she would come, and now that she was here, surrounded by the cheerful chatter of people who all knew each other, she felt like an outsider.

"Oh, Clara, you made it," Janice said, appearing at her side, her pink hair bobbing as she bounced excitedly. "We saved you a seat up front. Ted's doing a cello solo tonight. He's nervous as a cat in a room full of rocking chairs."

Without even waiting for a response, Janice linked arms with Clara and pulled her through to the row of chairs near the small stage. Frank and Emmy Lou were already sitting there and waved as they spotted her.

"Well, we didn't expect to see you here," Frank said. "I'm glad you came out."

Clara smiled. "Danielle suggested that I attend, maybe to get an idea of the musical talent on the island for wedding planning," she added very quickly.

Emmy Lou nodded. "Planning, schmanning. You know you're a part of our island now, honey. That means you show up for things whether you want to or not."

Before Clara could say anything, the lights dimmed, and Morty ran onto the stage wearing a sparkly purple bow tie.

"Ladies and gentlemen, welcome to our Wisteria Talent Showcase," he said, holding his arms up like a ringmaster. "We have a delightful lineup tonight, starting with our very own Ted, performing Bach's Cello Suite No. 1."

The audience clapped as Ted took to the stage, looking pale and clutching his cello like it was a shield. He sat in a chair, took a deep breath, and began to play.

Clara was surprised. His technique was perfect.

She could hear the small moments where nerves made his fingers slip or his bowing falter. The Bach Suite had been one of her husband's favorite pieces to conduct, and hearing it now brought both pain and pleasure.

When Ted finished, Clara applauded along with the crowd. He looked so relieved as he hurried off the stage and was soon replaced by a woman in her seventies who did a very limber tap dance routine.

The showcase continued, and Clara was struck by the different talents on display, from Dorothy reciting a dramatic monologue from one of her films to Gladys performing card tricks with her little dog as her assistant. The performances lacked technical perfection in most cases, but they made up for that with enthusiasm.

During a short intermission, Clara was surrounded by residents who were excited to meet her.

"So you're the conductor, right? What are you going to perform for us?" a man asked, who sported quite impressive mutton chops.

Clara felt panicked all of a sudden. "I'm not, actually. I haven't conducted since…"

"Oh, give her a chance to settle in," Janice chided.

"She did play beautifully with our little group the other day."

"You should play something tonight," Emmy Lou suggested, smiling brightly. "We have a pretty decent piano up there."

"Oh no, no, no, no. I couldn't possibly," Clara said, holding up her hands, but her fingers tingled with the memory of playing her own piano the other day.

"Of course she can't. She's not prepared," Ted said protectively. "Maybe next month's showcase."

Clara felt a rush of gratitude, but also a twinge of disappointment. Part of her, maybe a part she thought was long gone, actually wanted to play, to share the music that had been flowing through her fingers before.

She didn't even get a chance to reconsider before Morty was back on stage announcing the second half of the program. Clara sat back in her seat and listened as a quartet performed a slightly off-key rendition of "Blue Moon."

As the final performer finished - a retired English professor who juggled while reciting Shakespeare - Morty returned to make closing announcements.

"What a spectacular display of Wisteria talent. Before we close tonight, I received word that we have a surprise addition to our program. Our newest resident, the acclaimed conductor Clara Whitman, has graciously agreed to favor us with a piano performance."

Clara froze in shock. Everybody turned and looked at her. She hadn't agreed to any such thing. She glared at Janice, who grinned unrepentantly.

"I may have sent Morty a text," she said, whispering as low as she could. "Just go up there. One piece. Just play one piece. What's the worst thing that could happen?"

Clara was just about to refuse when she saw Danielle and Bennett walking into the back of the room. Danielle gave her an encouraging wave. Something inside Clara shifted.

These people had welcomed her, included her, and given her a space to grieve, but they were trying to encourage her to rejoin the living. Maybe it was time for her to take another step forward.

With a deep breath, she stood and slowly walked to the stage as people applauded enthusiastically. She sat at the piano and adjusted the bench, then took a moment to collect herself.

"I wasn't actually… I wasn't prepared for this," she said softly into the microphone.

She'd been in front of hundreds, sometimes

thousands of people, but right now she felt like a kid at her first recital.

"But music has been my best friend all my life, even when I tried to push it away at times. This piece is called 'Remember When,' and it was composed by my late husband, Robert."

Her fingers found the keys, and the gentle notes of Robert's composition filled the room. He'd written it during their 30th anniversary trip to Venice, inspired by the most perfect evening watching the sunset over the Grand Canal. The melody was wistful but also hopeful and very complex in structure.

Clara played, closing her eyes, letting the music carry her back to that time. For the first time since Robert's death, she played not just with technical precision but also with her whole heart and allowed the grief and love to flow out through her fingertips.

When the final notes faded, there was a moment of silence before the room erupted in applause.

Clara opened her eyes and found many of the audience members wiping away tears, including Dorothy, who seemed to be someone who rarely displayed emotion, especially publicly.

Danielle walked to the stage as Clara stood and offered her a hand, helping her down the steps.

"That was extraordinary, Clara. Thank you for sharing that with us."

"I really wasn't planning to," Clara whispered, "but somehow it felt right."

"Well, the best moments often come unplanned," Bennett said, joining them. "Your husband's composition was beautiful, as was your performance."

Clara found herself surrounded by residents, everyone offering appreciation for what she'd done. Even Cecilia approached and told her how much she admired the technical complexity of the song.

"You know," Morty said, "we've never had live music for our sunset gatherings at the beach, just that little portable speaker with spotty reception. Wouldn't it be lovely to have Clara play our keyboard out there occasionally?"

Clara immediately wanted to refuse, to retreat back into the safety of grief and solitude. But she felt such a warmth while playing, and such a connection to Robert's memory, it pulled her in a different direction.

"I think I might enjoy that," she said.

The crowd dispersed, and Clara found herself walking back to her cottage with a lightness in her step. The grief was still there; it would always be there, but tonight she learned that she could coexist with the grief.

When she got to her cottage, she went straight to the piano and lifted the stack of her husband's compositions she'd brought with her but hadn't been able to face. It was time to bring his music back to the world. It's what Robert would have wanted, and perhaps, she realized, it was what she needed as well.

Danielle woke up to the sound of hammering. Blurry-eyed, she looked over at her clock. 7:15 a.m. She groaned and pushed herself up, trudging to the window. She pulled back the curtain like she was an investigator looking for the source of the disturbance.

Off in the distance, at the bluff overlooking the cove, she saw a flurry of activity. Workers were wearing hard hats and moving things around a construction site, unloading materials from a big white truck, while others appeared to be measuring and marking the ground.

It was the gazebo project. Bennett had mentioned the builders were starting today, but she hadn't expected them to begin so early in the morning.

Her phone buzzed on the table with a text from Bennett.

Sorry about the noise. Brought a crew over on the first boat. Want to come see the progress after your morning rounds?

Smiling, she texted him back.

Only if you bring coffee. The GOOD kind from the mainland.

His response was immediate.

Deal. And I'll also throw in your favorite chocolate croissant. Meet you at 11?

Danielle put her phone down and walked over to the shower, suddenly excited despite the early wake-up call. The gazebo wasn't just going to be a wedding venue. It was going to be the symbol of their future together, a permanent addition to the island they both loved so much.

She got dressed and grabbed a quick breakfast before heading to the clinic for her morning appointments. Mrs. Henderson needed her blood pressure checked again, and Ted was due for his quarterly physical. These were routine matters that grounded her day-to-day life on the island.

As she walked toward the clinic, she saw her mother walking briskly along the path, dressed in workout clothes and looking kind of casual.

"Mom? You're up early."

Cecilia paused and wiped a fine sheen of perspiration from her brow. "Oh, good morning, dear. I've just been exploring your little island. The walking paths are quite lovely at dawn."

Danielle blinked in surprise. Her mom had never been one for casual exercise. Her fitness routine in New York always involved personal training sessions or Pilates classes with celebrities.

"Wait, you were, like, hiking voluntarily?"

Cecilia laughed, a light sound that reminded Danielle of those rare carefree moments from her childhood. "Oh, don't look so shocked. I'm not completely set in my ways." She gestured toward the gazebo under construction. "I see construction's underway. Bennett certainly doesn't waste time."

"He's very efficient," Danielle said. "And when he decides something is important, he makes it happen."

"That's a quality I've come to admire about him," Cecilia admitted. "You know, I've been thinking about the gazebo designs. The current plans are lovely, but I wonder if we might incorporate some lighting elements within the structure. You know, something subtle that could transition from daylight ceremony to an evening reception."

Danielle stared at her mother. "You're… you're, like, really getting into this island wedding idea, aren't you?"

Cecilia smoothed her hair. "Well, I mean, once I accepted that you weren't going to come to New York City, I decided I needed to make the best of it. I will say there's a certain charm to this place. Besides, it's on an island. That doesn't mean it can't be memorable and elegant."

Impulsively, Danielle hugged her mother. "Thank you for trying. And for being so open about doing things differently."

Cecilia returned the embrace, awkwardly patting her daughter's back. "Well, yes, your happiness is what matters, after all." She stepped back. "Now, I know you have patients waiting, and I'm meeting Dorothy for breakfast so we can discuss the centerpieces. That woman has surprising taste for someone who wears sunglasses indoors."

As her mother continued on her way, Danielle shook her head. Wisteria Island was definitely working its magic again. Cecilia Wright, renowned epidemiologist and Manhattan socialite, was power-walking at dawn and planning beach decorations with a retired movie star.

The clinic day passed quickly, and at eleven,

Danielle locked up, put a sign on the door, and headed toward the gazebo.

She saw Bennett before he saw her. He was standing at the edge of the marked foundation, deep in conversation with one of the contractors. The morning sun caught the little bits of red in his dark hair, and his hands moved as he explained something in an animated fashion. He was pointing at various areas of the site.

She couldn't help but feel a wave of love wash over her. This man could run a tech empire from afar, and yet chose to take big parts of his day involving himself in every aspect of island life.

"Is that my coffee I see?" she called as she approached.

Bennett turned, his face lighting up at the sight of her. "Ah, you're right on time. One large vanilla latte and a chocolate croissant, as promised." He handed her the treats and leaned in for a quick kiss. "So, what do you think?"

Danielle looked around where concrete footings were already being prepared. "It's happening fast."

"Oh, Miguel's crew is the best. They understand when something is urgent." He put his arm around her waist. "I want you to be able to stand in it and really feel what it will be like on our wedding day."

"At this rate, we could get married next month," Danielle joked, taking a sip of her coffee.

He looked at her with a sudden seriousness. "Hey, why not?"

"What?"

"Why not next month? Once the gazebo is complete, what are we really waiting for?"

Danielle blinked, caught off guard. "I mean, I just thought we'd have a longer engagement. Most weddings take months to plan and—"

"Do we need months?" Bennett interrupted. "We know we're getting married. We know where we're getting married. We know who's coming. They all live here. Morty and your mother have practically planned every detail. Why wait?"

Danielle thought about it. The truth was she'd been thinking of a longer engagement just out of convention, more than desire. She'd been married to her career for so long that she'd internalized the idea that big life decisions took extensive lead time. But standing there with Bennett, watching their wedding venue take a physical form, she felt only certainty. There really wasn't any reason to wait.

"Okay, let's do it," she said suddenly. "When the gazebo is finished, why not?"

Bennett smiled. "Really?"

"Really." She set her coffee down on a stack of wood and wrapped her arms around his neck. "I don't need a long engagement or a bunch of planning time. I just need you."

He kissed her then, a full kiss of promise and joy, not caring at all that a construction crew was a few yards away.

"Should we tell the others?" Danielle asked when they finally broke apart.

Bennett laughed. "And deny Morty the pleasure of planning for months on end? Oh, it seems cruel."

"True. But he's probably designed our first anniversary party already."

They stood together watching the work, Bennett's arm around her shoulders, Danielle's around his waist.

"My mother seems to be coming around," Danielle said. "I saw her this morning in workout clothes of all things, coming back from hiking around the island. She's apparently meeting Dorothy to discuss centerpieces right now."

Bennett smiled. "Wisteria has that effect on people. You know, it grows on you."

"Yeah, like a certain island owner I know," she said, squeezing his waist.

"Is that a complaint, Nurse Wright?"

"Not at all, Mr. Alexander. Not at all."

Cecilia sat alone on the bench overlooking the gazebo construction site. She pressed a handkerchief discreetly against her temple. The momentary dizziness had passed, but the headache was still lingering. It was the third one this week. She took a couple of slow breaths, willing the pain to subside before anybody noticed.

"Mom, are you all right?"

Cecilia straightened immediately and tucked the handkerchief back into her pocket as her daughter approached. "Oh, I'm fine, darling. Just taking a minute to appreciate the view." She gestured toward the gazebo where workers were installing the railing.

Danielle sat down beside her and studied her mother's face. "You're pale, and why are you squinting against the light?"

"Well, it's bright today," Cecilia said. "I forgot my sunglasses."

"Mm-hmm," Danielle murmured. "You know, you've been forgetting a lot of things lately, like you never mentioned why you canceled your keynote at the Nashville conference next month."

Cecilia frowned. "And how did you find out about that?"

"Dr. Patel mentioned it. Apparently, she was looking forward to hearing you speak." She turned toward her mother. "What is going on? And don't you tell me nothing. I've been a nurse long enough to know when someone's hiding symptoms."

For a minute, Cecilia considered maintaining the ruse. She'd spent her whole life presenting strength, never weakness. But there was something about Danielle staring directly into her eyes. It was so like her father when he wasn't being forthright with him.

"Look, I've just had a few headaches," she said, making her tone sound dismissive. "Probably tension from all the wedding planning. It's certainly nothing to concern yourself with, especially not right now."

"How frequent? Do they come with dizziness or vision changes?"

Cecilia sighed. "Yes, to the dizziness occasionally. No visual disturbances. And my blood pressure was a bit elevated at my last checkup, though my doctor didn't seem overly concerned."

"And when was this checkup?"

"Three months ago."

"Mom! And you haven't followed up?"

"Well, I've been a little busy with your wedding, if you haven't noticed." Her tone was sharper than she intended. She softened, reaching for Danielle's hand. "Look, I'm fine. Once this wedding's over, I'll make an appointment."

Danielle was quiet for a long moment. "I want to take your blood pressure now at the clinic. Please."

Cecilia recognized the mixture of professional concern and daughterly worry. "And will that set your mind at ease?"

"It would be a start."

"Okay, fine," Cecilia said, rising from the bench. She walked with deliberate steadiness despite having another wave of dizziness that she wouldn't tell Danielle about. "I have to check in with Dorothy about the orchid delivery first. She'll be impossible if I miss our appointment."

"The orchids can wait ten minutes," Danielle said firmly, taking her mother's arm.

They walked toward the clinic, and Cecilia found herself grateful for her daughter, but would never admit it out loud. The headaches had been worsening, and the dizziness was becoming a bit concerning, even to her scientifically objective mind. But the wedding was less than three weeks away. Whatever might be happening with her health would just have to wait until after her daughter's special day.

She wasn't going to allow anything, least of all her own body's inconvenient timing, to overshadow her daughter's happiness.

Danielle wrapped the blood pressure cuff around her mom's arm, trying to maintain some kind of professional detachment even though she was growing quite concerned. Cecilia sat perfectly still on the examination table, her posture as impeccable as ever, despite the paleness of her skin.

"Deep breath," Danielle said, inflating the cuff and watching the gauge.

As the reading became clear, she kept her expression neutral.

"165 over 90."

"That's a little bit high, isn't it?" Cecilia said, as if they were discussing someone else entirely.

"It's significantly elevated, Mom. How long have you been having these headaches?"

Cecilia considered for a moment. "About three weeks, I suppose."

"And the dizziness?"

"More recent. Maybe a week?"

Danielle made notes in a fresh chart. "Chest pain? Shortness of breath?"

"None," Cecilia said, smoothing an invisible wrinkle on her linen pants. "You know, I'm sure it's just stress and all this wedding planning. I haven't been sleeping well in the guest cottage. The mattress is firmer than what I'm used to."

Danielle knew deflection when she heard it. "Mom, hypertension at these levels is concerning. It's not something we can just dismiss as wedding stress, especially since it's been going on for a while."

"Yes, I'm well aware of the implications, Danielle," she said with a hint of irritation. "I did complete medical school, you know."

"Then you also know you need medication to bring your blood pressure down and further testing to make sure there's no underlying causes."

Cecilia stood and reached for her handbag. "And I'll consult with my physician when I return to New York after the wedding."

"Mom…"

"I won't have your special day disrupted

because of my medical issues," she said firmly. "And I feel perfectly fine. I'm more than capable of monitoring my condition for the next couple of weeks."

Danielle recognized the stubborn set of her mother's jaw. "At least let me get a doctor to prescribe something to lower it in the meantime. And you need to rest more. Reduce your sodium intake and take regular breaks throughout the day."

"Fine," Cecilia said. "Get a prescription if it will ease your mind. But not a word of this to Bennett or anyone else. The focus needs to remain on your wedding and not on my minor health concerns."

"They're not minor."

"Well, they're manageable," Cecilia said. "Dear, please, I've waited so long to see you this happy and to be a part of your special day. Don't let this little medical hiccup overshadow that."

Danielle sighed, knowing that she wasn't going to win the argument. "I'll get the prescription, but promise you'll take it as directed. And that you'll tell me immediately if your symptoms get worse."

"I promise. Doctor's honor."

She made a mental note to check on her mother more frequently in the coming days. She knew Cecilia was reluctant to become the center of attention. But elevated blood pressure combined with headaches and dizziness worried her a lot.

For now, though, she would respect her mother's wishes. The medication would help. Maybe she would rest and reduce some of her wedding duties enough to get her blood pressure down.

But as she watched her mother depart the clinic with her characteristic poise and grace, she couldn't shake the feeling that something serious might be brewing beneath her mother's perfect composure.

CHAPTER 7

Morty looked anxiously through Dorothy's window, watching the sky with concern on his face. Dark clouds were rolling in from the east, and the weather app on his phone showed this giant, ominous mass of green and yellow mixed with red moving toward the island.

"Well, it's going to rain," he said mournfully. "A lot by the looks of it."

Dorothy looked up from the table where she and Cecilia were arranging fabric swatches.

"Of course it is, darling. It's June in South Carolina. Afternoon thunderstorms are practically mandatory."

"But what about the gazebo being constructed?" Morty said, fretting. "They've only just started, and now they'll have to stop for days. It's going to delay everything."

"Concrete needs time to cure," Cecilia said. "A day's pause won't significantly impact the timeline."

Morty sighed dramatically and flopped onto Dorothy's emerald green velvet sofa. "I just don't handle setbacks well."

"Yes, we've noticed," Dorothy drawled, looking at Cecilia with amusement.

The three had fallen into an unexpected routine over the past week, meeting daily to plan different aspects of the wedding. What had started as a power struggle had turned into a surprisingly effective collaboration.

"Now, about the table arrangements," Cecilia continued. "I think we should group the residents by their interests instead of trying to do a traditional seating chart. I think it's more in keeping with the community spirit of the island."

"Just brilliant," Dorothy agreed. "Like, the book club members can sit together because they're quite boring. The card players can sit together because they're, well, quite annoying."

"And the beach walkers - the troublemakers," Morty added with a grin. "That table's probably going to be pretty large."

"And those nude beach people… well, maybe we don't invite them," Dorothy said, laughing. Cecilia looked at her with confusion.

A sharp crack of thunder punctuated his words, and he put his hand to his chest. A downpour came so suddenly and intensely that it obscured his view from the window. The rain hammered against the roof.

"My goodness," Cecilia said. "That is quite dramatic."

"Yes, weather tends to be theatrical here," Dorothy said. "Brief but intense performances, usually followed by an encore of sunshine."

Morty's phone buzzed with a text.

"It's Danielle," he said. "She and Bennett are stranded at the gazebo site. The rain started before they could make it back. So they've taken shelter in a construction trailer."

"How inconvenient," Cecilia said.

"Perhaps," Dorothy said with a mischievous glint in her eye. "Or maybe it's the universe arranging a romantic interlude for our lovebirds. Nothing like being trapped together during a storm."

"Dorothy!" Morty said, acting as though he was scandalized while he was really delighted. "They're already engaged."

"Engagement doesn't preclude romance, darling. Quite the opposite."

Cecilia laughed under her breath. "You know, it reminds me of how my husband proposed, actually. We were caught in a downpour in Central Park. Ended up sheltering in Belvedere Castle, soaking wet and laughing like a couple of fools. He proposed right there with no ring and no plan."

"You and your husband were married when he passed away?" Morty asked.

She laughed. "Oh no. We had been divorced for quite some time. I've found that sometimes the biggest romances turn into the biggest mistakes," Cecilia said, rolling her eyes. "Although I did get Danielle from that, so I can't say it was a mistake. But Harold was not the best husband to me, or any of the other wives he had after me."

Morty and Dorothy exchanged glances. In all of their planning sessions, Cecilia had rarely mentioned anything about her late husband, much less shared anything personal.

"Well, was your wedding grand?" Morty asked.

Cecilia shrugged her shoulders. "Not really. We were broke graduate students. Justice of the peace. Dinner at our favorite Italian restaurant with a few close friends. You know, I always told myself that

that was why I wanted something so elaborate for Danielle - to give her what I never had. But maybe what I had was perfect in its own way at the time."

"Well, love doesn't require grandeur," Dorothy said. "Though it certainly deserves celebration."

"When do you have to get back to New York?" Morty asked.

"Honestly, I took a bit of a leave of absence."

"Oh, Danielle didn't tell us that," Morty said.

"She doesn't know. I didn't want to worry her, but I decided to take some time off. I'm getting older, you know. I don't want to miss out on these moments. So I can stay here pretty much as long as I want."

"Oh, well, that's wonderful," Morty said.

"Anyway, this is why we will need to make this island wedding as special as possible. I mean, even if it's not at The Plaza." She straightened her shoulders. "Now, about the music - Clara said she has several musicians in mind. But we'll need to discuss the amplification of sound, given the outdoor setting."

Morty allowed her to change the subject, recognizing the significance of all that she'd shared. Cecilia Wright was showing them glimpses of the woman behind the polished exterior.

The rain continued to pound against the roof,

but inside Dorothy's cottage, they continued their happy little planning committee. Morty found himself hoping the storm might last just a little longer to give Danielle and Bennett their moment of shelter together, and give the three of them the quiet interlude of the unexpected connections they shared.

Bennett watched Danielle as she perched on a stack of lumber in the construction trailer and wrung water from her hair. They were both soaked from the sudden downpour, but she was still breathtakingly beautiful, even with tousled curls and flushed cheeks.

"Well, I guess this is cozy," she said, pointing around the cramped trailer filled with tools and building materials. "It's not exactly the romantic afternoon I had in mind, but I guess it has a certain rustic charm."

Bennett laughed and took off his equally soaked jacket. "Well, if by rustic charm you mean the distinct aroma of sawdust and Miguel's lunch leftovers, then I guess, yeah, it's pretty charming."

Rain hammered against the metal roof and

created a deafening backdrop to their conversation. Wind occasionally gusted against the small window, driving rain sideways in sheets.

"Do you think the foundation will be okay?" Danielle asked, looking out at the construction site, where tarps flapped wildly over freshly poured concrete.

"I told you, Miguel knows exactly what he's doing. Anybody who builds anything in a coastal area knows how to protect things from the weather." Bennett moved a blueprint and sat beside her on the lumber pile. "Besides, I think I heard that rain at the beginning of a project is supposed to be good luck."

"Is that a real superstition, or did you just make that up?"

"Maybe a little of both," he said, shrugging. "But I choose to believe it right now."

Thunder cracked in the distance, making them both jump. Danielle laughed, leaning against him.

"You know, I haven't been caught in a storm like this since I was a kid at summer camp. I remember one time we had to huddle in the mess hall for hours."

"Well, that sounds traumatic."

"Actually, it was kind of magical. The counselors made up games, and someone found a guitar. By the time the storm passed, we'd made a bunch of new friends. You know, it's funny how being stuck somewhere can create unexpected memories."

Bennett slipped his arm around her shoulders. "Oh, you mean like being stranded on a small island and falling in love with the local nurse?"

She smiled at him. "Exactly like that."

Another crack of thunder, followed by a brilliant flash of lightning, illuminated the trailer in stark white light. The rain intensified.

"Well, it looks like we might be here for a little while," Bennett said. "Any idea how you want to pass the time?"

"We could start planning our honeymoon," Danielle said. "You still haven't told me where we're going."

"Well, that's because it's a surprise."

"Not even a hint? Just tell me the continent. Or the climate. Or do I need to take my passport?"

Bennett pretended to consider it, but he wasn't about to tell her anything. "It's somewhere beautiful, with you. That's all you need to know."

She poked him in the ribs. "You're impossible."

"Well, you knew that when you agreed to marry me."

"You know, there is something we should probably discuss, since we have this unexpected private time."

He raised an eyebrow. "Well, that sounds pretty ominous."

"Not ominous, but important. Something we probably should have talked about more by now." She took in a deep breath. "Do you still want children?"

"Yes, of course," he said. "I've always wanted a family. But I wasn't sure if you still… You know, with your career and on the island…"

"I do," Danielle said, meeting his eyes. "I always assumed I'd have children one day, but my career took priority. And then my ex…" She shook her head. "Let's just say I stopped planning for it. With him, anyway. But being here and seeing how much you care about everyone on this island and how you've created a community… I want to build a family with you, Bennett."

His heart swelled. He pulled her closer, pressing a kiss to her temple.

"You're going to be an amazing mother."

"And you'll be a wonderful father. Can you imagine raising little ones here on the island, surrounded by a hundred grandparents? I think we might need to get a bigger house, though. The cottage is perfect for me, but a baby?"

"Well, we could build something new or expand your place. Whatever you want."

Danielle smiled. "We have time to figure that out."

"Well, not as much as you think," Bennett said. "I mean, if we're getting married next month and starting a family soon after…"

"Hey, let's not get ahead of ourselves," Danielle laughed. "One major life event at a time, if you don't mind."

The rain started to ease slightly.

"Sounds like the storm might be passing," Bennett said.

He made no move to get up. Spending this alone time with her was perfect, and these times together without somebody popping in were few and far between. She seemed to feel the same, curling in closer to his side.

"Oh, a few more minutes won't hurt," she said. "I'm comfortable right where I am."

He tightened his arm around her, filled with a contentment that had nothing to do with where they were, but everything to do with the woman sitting beside him.

Here in this ratty construction trailer with rain drumming on the roof, he had everything he could ever want - Danielle, a plan for their future, and a certainty that no matter what storms might come, they would weather them together, side by side.

C lara stood at the edge of the water and watched as the sun rose over the Atlantic. She loved taking these early morning walks along the shore. There was something about the rhythm of the waves and the gradual lightening of the sky that gave her solace.

Two weeks had passed since her impromptu performance at the talent show. Two weeks of small, steady steps back toward the living. She'd played at three of the sunset gatherings on the beach and brought her husband's compositions to life. She continued working with the Wisteria Philharmonic, guiding them towards greater cohesion, and she'd started working on wedding music with Danielle and Bennett, choosing pieces that would be complementary to their ceremony in the nearly completed gazebo.

The gazebo. Clara smiled when she thought of

the structure taking shape over on the bluff. Despite the early rainstorm delay, Miguel's crew had worked quickly and efficiently, and now the framework stood proud against the sky with its clean lines and graceful proportions. Yesterday, they had started installing the roof, and soon all the finishing details would transform it from a construction site into a wedding venue.

She saw some movement down the beach that caught her eye, another early riser taking advantage of a beautiful morning. Then she recognized Bennett's frame as he jogged along the water's edge. He waved when he spotted her and stopped as she approached.

"Good morning, Clara. Beautiful sunrise today, isn't it?"

"Absolutely stunning," she said, "although I didn't expect to find the island's owner out running at dawn. Don't you have people to do that sort of thing for you?"

Bennett laughed. "I've always been an early riser. There's something about seeing the island wake up that just centers me for the day ahead."

Clara nodded. "The gazebo's coming along nicely. Cecilia really added some beautiful design elements to make it elegant."

"She has excellent taste," Bennett said, "and a surprising knowledge of architectural details. The wedding's in less than three weeks, you know. We moved up the date once we realized how quickly the gazebo would be completed."

"So I've heard. Morty is in an absolute tizzy trying to speed up all his planning."

"Oh, Morty exists in a permanent state of tizzy from what I've seen over the years," Bennett said. "But his heart's in the right place."

They turned and watched a pair of sandpipers darting along the water's edge.

"Listen, I wanted to thank you," Bennett said, "for agreeing to play at the wedding. It means a lot to Danielle, well, to both of us."

"Oh, it's my pleasure. Music for a wedding should be as unique as the couple themselves, and it's giving me a purpose."

"You seem a little lighter these days, if you don't mind me saying so."

Clara nodded. "I think I am. The weight doesn't disappear, but somehow it becomes more bearable. Like I'm building up a muscle through repeated use."

"Grief is strength training," Bennett said.

"That's a perspective I haven't heard before, but it fits. I think here on Wisteria Island, what I've seen happen to people is that when they don't have to carry that grief alone anymore, they realize they can carry it with a group of people, and it makes everything lighter."

"I'm a work in progress for sure," Clara said. "Some days are better than others, but this place…" she gestured toward the island behind them. "It helps. All these people have helped, and I really didn't think that was possible."

"That's what I hoped to create here," he said. "A place of healing and connection. My grandmother used to say the worst thing about growing old wasn't the physical limitations. It was the loneliness, the feeling of being forgotten or irrelevant."

"She sounded like a wise woman."

"She was. I wish…" he paused. "I wish she could have seen this place. I wish she could have lived here. But I was far too young when she passed away. I couldn't help her, but I can help other people. Or at least I hope I'm helping." He glanced at his watch. "Well, I should finish my run. Contractors arrive at eight."

Clara nodded. "I promised to help Janice with something called chair yoga this morning. Apparently, my 'excellent posture' makes me qualified as an assistant instructor."

Bennett laughed. "Welcome to island life, where everyone's talents get repurposed in all the most unexpected ways." He started to jog in place, preparing to continue his run. "Oh, and before I forget, Danielle mentioned you were having some issues with your piano. Something about the humidity affecting the tuning?"

Clara sighed. "Yeah, unfortunately. It's an occupational hazard of coastal living, I suppose. I've called a tuner from the mainland, but they can't come until next week."

"I might be able to help with that," Bennett said. "My mom was a piano teacher for a long time. I learned to tune by ear out of necessity. We couldn't afford a professional when I was a kid. Not all my skills are business-related," he said with a wink.

"Well, I wouldn't want to impose."

"It's not an imposition. Besides, Danielle's at a medical conference on the mainland until this evening. I could use the distraction."

"Well, that would be wonderful. The wedding music really needs to be practiced on a properly tuned instrument."

"So, this afternoon? Maybe around two?"

"Oh, perfect. I'll bake you some cookies as payment."

Bennett laughed. "Deal."

With a final wave, he continued his run down the beach, disappearing around a bend into the coastline.

Clara looked back toward her cottage, feeling anticipation for the day ahead. It had been months since she'd woken up looking forward to anything, but today she had chair yoga with Janice, lunch with Dorothy, who wanted to discuss music for some mysterious wedding surprise, and now Bennett's visit to tune her piano.

A full day. A good day.

She walked home in the strengthening sunlight and found herself humming one of Robert's melodies. It was a piece he'd written after they spent a summer in Provence, full of light and warmth. For the first time, the music brought more comfort than pain.

CHAPTER 8

Danielle adjusted her dress as she waited in the lobby of the Atlanta hotel where her mother was staying during a brief professional conference. They had planned this lunch weeks ago, before Cecilia's visit to the island and before the wedding planning had brought them together again.

The elegant restaurant was a far cry from the cafeteria on Wisteria Island, with its crisp white tablecloths and hovering waitstaff. Danielle used to go to places like this all the time, but now she felt slightly out of place in her simple sundress.

"Danielle, darling!"

She turned to see Cecilia walking toward her, looking every inch the distinguished professional in her tailored navy dress and pearls.

"Mom, you look wonderful," Danielle said, hugging her. "How was your panel this morning?"

"Interesting, though the moderator could have managed his time better. He's a virologist from Johns Hopkins, and he went seven minutes over his allotted time." Cecilia rolled her eyes. "But enough about academia. Let's sit. I have been looking forward to this all day."

They were shown to a table by the window overlooking the hotel's manicured gardens. After ordering, Cecilia stuck to her usual niçoise salad, and Danielle opted for the special. They fell into conversation about wedding plans again.

"So, Dorothy and I found the perfect linens the other day," Cecilia started. "A subtle pattern. It complements the floral arrangements without competing with them. And Morty has hired some young fella from the mainland to handle lighting. Apparently, he does work in film production in Savannah."

Danielle smiled, still getting used to her mother's enthusiasm for an island wedding. "It sounds like everything's coming together. I've barely had to lift a finger."

"Indeed, though I still think your timeline's

pretty rushed. Three weeks sure doesn't leave much margin for error."

"Well, Bennett and I don't see any reason to wait," Danielle said. "The gazebo will be finished, the plans are in place, and honestly, Mom, I'm just ready to be his wife."

"You really do love him, don't you?"

"With all my heart."

Cecilia reached across the table to squeeze her daughter's hand. "I'm glad. Although your father and I didn't work out in the end, we had that kind of love. The kind that makes you impatient to begin forever together."

Danielle felt a lump form in her throat. Her mother rarely spoke about her father after the divorce.

"I wish he could be here," Danielle said quietly.

She'd been afraid to say it before, not wanting to upset her mother, but she did wish that her father could walk her down the aisle.

"He will be there in his own way," Cecilia said. "Actually, it's something I wanted to discuss with you."

She reached into her very expensive handbag and took out a small velvet box.

"I brought this from New York. I thought maybe you might want to wear it at your wedding."

She opened the box to reveal a delicate sapphire and diamond bracelet.

"Your father gave this to me on our tenth wedding anniversary. 'Something blue,' he called it, to make up for the wedding jewelry that we couldn't afford when we got married."

"Mom, it's beautiful. But are you sure?"

"Oh, absolutely sure. What do I need it for? It would mean a great deal to me if you'd wear it. It's a way for him to be a part of your day. Oh, Danielle, he would have been so proud of the woman you've become. The way that you care for others, and the way you've created life on your own terms."

Danielle's eyes welled with tears. "Even though I didn't become a research physician like you wanted?"

Cecilia looked down at her newly manicured hands and then looked back at Danielle.

"I wanted you to follow in my footsteps because I knew that path. I understood it. I felt like I could keep you safe. But you found your own way. A better way for you. And seeing you on that island with those people who absolutely adore you, and Bennett, well, now I understand that you made the right choice."

"Thank you. That means more to me than you know."

The server arrived with their meals, and when he departed, Cecilia carefully closed the velvet box and passed it across the table.

"Something blue," she said simply. "And something from your father."

Danielle took the box and held it to her chest.

"Thank you. I'll treasure it."

They ate in silence for a few moments before Cecilia spoke again.

"So, I've been meaning to ask you, what are your plans for the clinic while you're on your honeymoon? Bennett said you might have to do interviews for temporary coverage."

"Actually, yes. We do have another doctor, Zach, who works on the island, but he's on leave right now. His mother has been ill. But Dr. Patel from Savannah General said that she can come because she's between positions and looking for something short-term. So she'll come to the island next week to meet the residents and learn the systems."

"Oh, that's excellent. I'm sure continuity of care is very important in a place like that. And afterward, will you be staying in your cottage or moving in with Bennett?"

"We'll stay in my place for now. It's smaller, but I love it so much. And Bennett's is more… utilitarian," she said, laughing. "Eventually, we'll build something together. Something with room to grow."

"To grow? Are you planning to expand the clinic?"

"Not exactly," Danielle took in a deep breath. "Bennett and I want children. Not right away, but soon."

For a moment, Cecilia sat there perfectly still, and then her face transformed with such joy that Danielle was stunned.

"Grandchildren," she whispered, as if she was testing out the word against her tongue. "Oh, Danielle."

"So you're happy about this?"

"Darling, of course! Why wouldn't I be?" Cecilia said, clapping her hands together.

"I guess I thought you might worry about my career. Or being isolated on the island."

"Family comes first," Cecilia said firmly. "It always has, or at least, it always should have, even when I wasn't good at showing it. And as for isolation, well, I'll simply have to visit more often, won't

I? Maybe when my hair starts to go gray, I'll get a little cottage on Wisteria Island myself. And I need to introduce the children to the finer things in life, like a proper ballet and museum exhibitions."

Danielle laughed, trying to imagine her mother living on Wisteria Island. "You're never going to let your hair go gray. But I'd love for you to be around. I want my kids to know their grandmother."

"And I should know them." Cecilia's eyes grew distant. "Your father would have been a wonderful grandfather. Despite what happened with our marriage, he always had more patience than I did."

As their lunch continued, Cecilia shared stories about Danielle's father that she'd never heard—his terrible cooking attempts, his love of jazz clubs, the time he got them lost in rural France because he refused to ask for directions.

Danielle felt a new connection forming with her mother and her late father, and it felt good.

When they parted ways outside the restaurant, Cecilia hugged her daughter tightly. "I'll see you back on the island in a few days. Can you please try to keep Morty from adding disco balls to the gazebo before I return?"

Danielle laughed. "No promises."

Morty was in crisis mode. Complete, utter, unmitigated crisis mode.

"Oh my goodness, it's a disaster," he moaned, pacing Dorothy's living room while wringing his hands dramatically. "It's a complete and total catastrophe."

Dorothy lounged elegantly on her chaise, removed her sunglasses, and looked at him with a pointed stare.

"Darling, unless someone has died or the island is sinking into the ocean, I suggest you dial back the theatrics. You're giving me a migraine," she said, rubbing her temples.

"The wedding flowers!" Morty wailed. "The supplier just called. They can't get the exact orchid variety we ordered, the one that Cecilia was adamant about. Something about a tropical storm devastating a greenhouse," he said, waving his hand in the air. "They've offered substitutions, but they simply won't be the same!"

Dorothy sighed. "Is that all? For heaven's sake, Morty, I thought something truly terrible had happened."

"This is truly terrible. The cascading orchids are

the centerpiece of our gazebo design. You know, Cecilia specifically only approved that particular shade of blush."

"Cecilia is a rational, educated woman who will understand that acts of God and nature are beyond our control," Dorothy said calmly. "Now sit down before you wear a hole in my prized Persian rug."

Morty collapsed onto the sofa. "Everything that was going to be so perfect is gone. I'll be the laughingstock of Wisteria Island if I can't pull this thing off without a hitch."

Dorothy studied her friend. "You know what your problem is, Morty? You've lost perspective. This wedding isn't about the perfect flowers or certain color schemes. It's about our Danielle and Bennett declaring their undying love for each other."

"But…"

"No buts. They would marry in a thunderstorm wearing potato sacks if that were their only option. These details only matter to us, not to them."

Morty's shoulders slumped. "I just wanted everything to be perfect. They deserve it after everything they've done for us. They should have the most perfect day."

"Oh, my dear, perfect doesn't exist. Not even in Hollywood. Believe me, I've seen enough movie magic to know everything's smoke and mirrors." She stood up and sat down beside him. "But you know what does exist? Love. Community. Joy. And this wedding will have those in abundance. Orchids or no orchids."

"I suppose," Morty conceded.

"Besides," Dorothy said, smiling, "I happen to know that Clara's cousin manages the botanical garden near Charleston. It has a renowned orchid collection. One call from me could persuade him to part with a few specimens for a worthy cause."

Morty's head snapped toward her. "Really? You would do that?"

"Darling, I'm Dorothy Monroe. I was seducing orchids from botanical gardens long before you were born."

She patted his knee. "Let me make a call."

Dorothy swept off to retrieve her phone, and Morty felt his panic subsiding slightly. Of course, Dorothy was right. The wedding would be beautiful no matter what kind of setbacks they had. But if he was being honest with himself, a part of his distress came from knowing that once the wedding was over, his role in island life might diminish again.

Planning the wedding had made him feel important and given him purpose, a reason for people to seek his input. As boisterous and extroverted as Morty was, he craved connection with other people, and sometimes he felt like he didn't get enough of it. What would happen when the gazebo emptied and the guests went home, and he was left to feel alone again?

Dorothy returned, looking triumphant.

"Well, it's arranged. Clara's cousin William will personally select and deliver a collection of premium orchids two days before the wedding. Crisis averted," she said, putting her sunglasses back on.

"Dorothy, you're a miracle worker."

"Yes, I'm aware," she said dryly. "Now, can we discuss more pressing matters, like the fact that your bow tie collection doesn't include anything in that exact shade of sea foam that we're using for the bridesmaids' bouquets?"

Morty gasped in horror. "Oh my gosh, you're right. I need to place a rush order immediately."

He pulled out his phone to remedy this critical fashion emergency and realized something important. The wedding might end, but the relationships he'd formed with those who had helped him plan it - like Dorothy and Danielle and Bennett, and all the residents of Wisteria Island who'd been involved - those would continue.

His place in the community didn't depend on planning the most perfect event. It was secure simply because he was finally in a place where he belonged.

The gazebo stood like a monument, gleaming in the morning light, with its white columns and graceful dome catching the sun's early rays. Two weeks of dedicated work had transformed it from a construction site into an elegant structure that looked like it had always been a part of the island.

Bennett walked around it slowly, inspecting every detail. The railings had been installed yesterday. The floor was finished with a natural cedar planking that would weather to a soft silver-gray over time. Inside, recessed lighting was strategically placed to illuminate the space for evening gatherings. It was in every way exactly what he had hoped for—a beautiful setting for their wedding and a lasting addition to the island they both loved.

"It's beautiful," came a voice from behind him.

Bennett turned to find Cecilia approaching, looking rested despite her recent trips away from the island for medical conferences.

"Thank you," he said. "Your design suggestions made it exceptional."

Cecilia walked around the gazebo. "Miguel's team executed all the details perfectly. These proportions are exactly right - elegant without being ostentatious."

"Well, that's high praise from someone with your eye for design," Bennett said.

She smiled. "Maybe in another life, I was an architect rather than an epidemiologist. I might have missed my calling."

"Well, it's never too late to explore new interests," Bennett said. "That's one of the principles Wisteria was founded on."

"Indeed," Cecilia said, running her hand along one of the smooth columns. "Have you shown Danielle yet?"

"Not the finished version. She's been busy with clinic duties and training Dr. Patel. I want to surprise her this evening once the landscaping is done."

They both turned at the sound of approaching footsteps. Eddie was leading a small team, carrying flats of flowering plants and bags of mulch.

"Morning, boss. Dr. Wright," he said, nodding at

Cecilia. "Ready to put the finishing touches on this beauty today."

"Well, perfect timing. I was just telling Cecilia about the landscaping plans."

Eddie gestured toward the plants. "Coastal natives mostly - sea lavender, beach roses, and some ornamental grasses that can handle the salty air. Plus wisteria, of course, to climb the trellises on either side. Come spring, this place will be draped in beautiful purple blooms."

"How appropriate," Cecilia nodded. "I particularly like the idea of planting something that will grow and mature along with their marriage."

Bennett hadn't thought of it that way, but the metaphor made him smile. "Exactly. Something beautiful that becomes something stronger with each passing year."

As Eddie's team began placing the plants according to the landscape designer's plan, Bennett and Cecilia moved over to a bench overlooking the site.

"You know, I had lunch with Danielle in Atlanta," Cecilia said.

"She mentioned it went well," Bennett replied.

"Better than well. We talked - really talked - for the first time in years." She paused. "She told me about your plans for a family," she said, turning to face him.

Bennett nodded. "Not immediately, but yes. We both want children."

"I'm glad. Nothing has brought me greater joy than being Danielle's mother, despite my… let's just say… imperfections in the role." She looked out toward the ocean. "Her father and I would have been overjoyed to know that we would have grandchildren someday. He always said Danielle would be a wonderful mother."

"She will be. And you'll be a wonderful grandmother."

Cecilia smiled. "I hope to be. I've been given a second chance with Danielle, and I don't intend to squander it."

They sat in silence for a while, watching the planting progress. Bennett found himself appreciating this new side of his future mother-in-law, the woman beneath the polished exterior who clearly loved her daughter, even though she hadn't always shown it in ways that Danielle could recognize.

"You know, I brought something for you too," Cecilia said, reaching into her handbag. She pulled out a small black box and handed it to Bennett. "This belonged to Danielle's father."

He opened it to find a pair of platinum cufflinks, simple but elegant, each inset with a small sapphire.

"They were his favorite. He wore them to every important occasion in our life together, and I'm sure afterward. I thought perhaps you might wear them for the wedding. A connection to Danielle's father, who would have been proud to welcome you to our family."

Bennett was momentarily speechless. "Cecilia, I'm honored. Truly."

"Good." She stood quickly, as if she was embarrassed by the emotional moment. "Now I should check on Morty. He has texted me seventeen times today during my flight about some orchid emergency that Dorothy apparently resolved. That man needs my constant supervision."

As she walked away, Bennett remained on the bench, the box of cufflinks warm in his palm. Her gift to him represented more than just a wedding accessory. It was an acceptance of him, a passing of a symbolic torch between Danielle's father and him, who would now be her partner through life.

CHAPTER 9

C lara sat at her piano and allowed her fingers to dance over the keys as she played through the processional music she had arranged for Danielle and Bennett's wedding. Of course, she wouldn't be playing on her own piano because they couldn't cart that out to the gazebo. She'd be using the community center keyboard, which wouldn't sound nearly the same, but would do in a pinch.

The piece she had created combined elements of classical tradition with more contemporary harmonies, creating something both timeless and fresh, just like the couple themselves.

She could hear it in her mind. The string quartet from Savannah that Bennett had hired would begin with a gentle introduction, and then Clara would join on the digital piano as Danielle began her walk down the aisle. The key change at precisely the moment she would reach Bennett would bring goosebumps to everyone present.

A knock at the door interrupted her playing. She set aside her music sheets and rose to answer it, finding Danielle on her porch with a large garment bag.

"I hope I'm not interrupting," Danielle said. "I heard you playing. It sounded beautiful."

"Just practicing for your big day," Clara said, stepping aside and letting her in. "Is everything okay?"

Danielle set the garment bag down carefully across a chair. "More than okay. The gazebo is finished. Bennett says the landscaping will be done tonight, and Morty's orchid crisis has apparently been averted by Dorothy. But I do need your help with something else important."

"Of course. What can I do?"

Danielle unzipped the garment bag to reveal a simple but elegant white gown. "I need an honest opinion from someone with good taste who isn't emotionally invested in the wedding planning. I just want to know - is this the right dress?"

Clara studied the gown. It was beautiful, clean,

and timeless - a sleeveless A-line with a sweetheart neckline and minimal embellishment.

"It's perfect. Elegant, flattering, entirely you. Isn't it a little late in the game to ask if it's okay?"

Danielle chuckled. "I suppose so, but I could still make it over to the mainland and get to a wedding shop if I had to. It seems most of the dresses fit someone my size. My mother helped me pick this one out, but I never know if something's too over the top when Cecilia Wright is involved."

"Well, it's perfect."

Danielle's relief was palpable. "Thank you. My mother wanted something a little more elaborate - some lace overlays, beading, a dramatic long train that half the island could ride on as I walked down the aisle. This was our compromise."

"And it was a successful one," Clara assured her. "You'll look stunning. The simplicity is going to be so striking in the gazebo setting."

Danielle smiled and re-zipped the garment bag. "That's what I hoped. Bennett always says I'm most beautiful when I'm most myself."

"He's a very wise man," Clara said.

"He is. So, how are you doing, really?"

Clara considered the question. "Better. Each day

is a little easier than the last. Playing music again has helped me the most."

"I've noticed a change in you," Danielle said. "There's a lightness that wasn't there when you first arrived here."

"Well, you know… the grief doesn't go away. It's a life sentence," Clara said. "I still miss my husband every day. But I'm learning that remembering him doesn't have to only be remembering pain. I can honor him through music, and really think about our memories together with a smile."

"That's a beautiful way to think about it."

"You know, he would have liked your Bennett. Robert always appreciated people who built things to last—whether it was music or communities."

"Well, I wish we could have met him."

"He'll be here in a way," Clara said, "in the music I've arranged and the pieces I'll play. A small part of him lives on in everything I create."

Danielle nodded. "You know, that's why I asked the pastor who will officiate the wedding for us to do a remembrance moment in the ceremony. For Bennett's grandmother, my father, and all of the people who have lost someone who live here on Wisteria Island. People who should be there but can only be with us in spirit."

"That's very meaningful," Clara said.

They sat together at the piano, and Clara showed Danielle the processional score, explaining how the music would flow throughout the ceremony. Two months ago, she couldn't have imagined sitting here planning wedding music without being overwhelmed by memories of her own marriage.

While the memories would always remain, they brought more comfort than pain now. She refused to remember her marriage as a sad thing and something she'd lost.

"Will you play something for me?" Danielle asked when they finished discussing the ceremony music. "Something of Robert's?"

Clara nodded and placed her hands on the keys. She chose one of Robert's later compositions, a piece he'd written after they celebrated their thirtieth anniversary.

As the final notes faded, Danielle wiped away a tear. "That was beautiful, Clara. Thanks for sharing it."

"Thank you for asking," Clara said. "For a long time, I couldn't bear to play his music. I wouldn't even pull out the pieces of paper and look at them. But now it feels like the most natural way to keep him with me. It's like he's right here beside me."

When Danielle left, promising to return later in the week for the final music rehearsal, Clara remained at the piano. She pulled out a blank sheet of staff paper and began to write, capturing a melody that had been forming in her mind for days. It would be a wedding gift for Danielle and Bennett —a brand-new composition, the first she had attempted since her husband's death. Not a replacement for his music, but something that grew alongside it.

Inspired by the new connections she had already formed on Wisteria Island, she felt her husband's presence not as a ghost, but as an inspiration, encouraging her, as he always had, to create beauty in the world—even in the face of grief.

Danielle tried to keep her eyes closed as Bennett led her up a slight incline. His hands were warm on her shoulders, guiding her forward.

"We're almost there," he said. "Just a few more steps. But you better not peek."

"I'm not," she said for the umpteenth time, though the temptation was very strong.

Of course, she'd seen the gazebo during the

construction, but Bennett had insisted on doing a final reveal as a surprise.

They stopped, and his hands left her shoulders. She heard him move to stand beside her.

"All right," he said. "Open your eyes."

Danielle did, and her breath caught in her throat.

The gazebo stood before her, gleaming white against the deepening twilight sky. Landscape lighting illuminated its beautiful columns and dome from below, and in the interior, it glowed with the soft radiance of hidden fixtures. Around its base, carefully arranged plants created a beautiful flowing transition from the surrounding landscape. Two curved benches flanked the wide entrance steps, and a path of crushed shell led to where they stood at the gazebo's opening.

But what made it truly magical was what was beyond it. It was positioned perfectly on the bluff, with the gazebo framing the ocean horizon. Tonight it was being painted in shades of purple and gold as the sun dipped behind the water.

"Oh my gosh, Bennett," she said. "It's perfect. Absolutely perfect. Better than any big cathedral or fancy wedding venue could have ever been."

He took her hand and led her up the shell path toward the structure. "Come see inside."

They climbed the three wide steps and entered the octagonal space. The cedar flooring gleamed beneath their feet, and the interior of the dome had been finished with a pale blue.

"It's like standing inside of a seashell," she said, turning around to take in the 360-degree view. "I just can't believe how beautiful this is."

"And this is where we'll stand," Bennett said, guiding her to the center of the space, positioning them to face the ocean view. "Right here. This is where we'll say our vows."

She could picture it clearly— all of their friends gathered around, Clara's music playing, the sunset sky creating the perfect backdrop as they committed the rest of their lives to each other.

"One more week," she said softly. "Just one more week."

Bennett wrapped his arms around her from behind and rested his chin on top of her head. "The longest week of my life," he said.

Danielle laughed. "Are you impatient, Mr. Alexander?"

"To make you my wife? Absolutely."

They stood together as the last light faded from the sky, and the stars emerged one by one above them. Danielle could hear the gentle sound of waves breaking against the shore below.

"I have something to tell you, too," she said after a while, turning in his arms to face him. "I picked up my wedding dress today."

His eyes lit up with interest. "And?"

"Oh, and you don't get to see it until next Saturday," she said, teasing. "But I will tell you that Clara approves, and I think she has pretty excellent taste."

"Well, if you're wearing it, I know it's already perfect," Bennett said, brushing a strand from her face. "You could wear one of Morty's flamingo shirts and still be the most beautiful bride in history."

Danielle laughed. "Don't you give him any ideas. He's already lobbying to add, 'just a touch of sequins' to these gazebo columns."

"Over my dead body," Bennett said, making her laugh harder.

As their laughter faded, they naturally moved into a slow dance, swaying together in the middle of the gazebo with no music, just the sound of the ocean breeze and distant waves. She rested her cheek against Bennett's chest, feeling the steady beat of his heart beneath her ear.

This was home, she realized. Not just Wisteria

Island. Not just her cottage or this beautiful gazebo. But here, in Bennett's arms, where she belonged.

"I love you," she whispered. "Thank you for building this. And I don't just mean the gazebo, but everything. This community, this life we share."

He tightened his arms around her. "Thank you for staying. For seeing what this place could be, and what we could be - together."

They continued their silent dance beneath a star-filled sky, and Danielle felt a sense of rightness wash over her. She knew that no matter what happened from here on out, she and Bennett would face everything together, supported by the remarkable family they'd built on Wisteria Island.

One week couldn't come soon enough.

The island was buzzing with pre-wedding activity. There were only three days to go before the wedding, and residents had thrown themselves into full preparation mode. Janice and her self-appointed flower committee were creating arrangements for the rehearsal dinner, while Ted and Frank had volunteered to set up chairs at the gazebo. Even Dorothy had rolled up her sleeves. Of course, that was metaphorically speaking—she wouldn't be caught dead without her signature silk blouses—but she was overseeing the transformation of the community center for the reception.

In the middle of the chaos, Morty paced anxiously outside Clara's cottage, his trusty clipboard in hand, muttering to himself. When Clara opened the door, he practically fell inside.

"Oh, thank goodness you're home. We have a situation," he said, throwing his free hand up in the air.

Clara, who had grown accustomed to Morty's "situations" over the past weeks, calmly pointed for him to sit. "Take a deep breath and tell me what's happened."

"It's the string quartet," he moaned. "The cellist broke her wrist in a bicycle accident yesterday. Ran over a turtle. Isn't that sad? Anyway, they found a replacement, but he hasn't rehearsed any of our arrangements. And apparently he reads music 'adequately at best,' according to the first violinist."

Clara tried to process all of the information Morty had spit out like a high-powered water hose. "That is challenging, but not insurmountable. When will they arrive on the island?"

"Tomorrow afternoon for the rehearsal."

"Perfect. I'll work with the new cellist separately before the full rehearsal. I'm sure we can simplify the part if necessary."

Morty looked at her with admiration. "You're not panicking? Why aren't you panicking? I'm panicking enough for both of us."

Clara smiled, surprised that indeed she wasn't panicking. A few months ago, this kind of last-minute complication might have sent her spiraling with anxiety, but now it felt like a problem that just needed to be solved.

"Music always comes with unexpected challenges," she said. "That's what makes a live performance so special. We'll adapt. Musicians know how to do that."

"Well, you're just a marvel, Clara Whitman," Morty said. "I don't know what we'd do without you. I'm so glad you came to Wisteria Island."

"Well, you'd probably hire a DJ and call it a day," she said dryly.

Morty clutched his chest in mock horror. "Blasphemy! This wedding deserves live music of the highest caliber." He looked at his clipboard. "Now, about the prelude selections…"

A knock at the door interrupted them. Clara

opened it to find Eddie holding a large, elegant box tied with a white ribbon.

"This is a delivery for you, Clara. Just arrived on the morning boat."

She took the box with surprise. "Thanks, Eddie, but I wasn't expecting anything."

Eddie departed, and Clara set the box on her coffee table and carefully untied the ribbon. Nestled inside tissue paper was a stunning silk wrap in a shade of deep blue that reminded her of twilight. A small card rested on top.

For our pianist extraordinaire, with gratitude for the music you've brought to our lives. —Danielle and Bennett

"Oh my," Morty said, looking over her shoulder. "That's exquisite. Italian silk by the look of that. And the color will be perfect with your hair."

Clara ran her fingers over the luxurious fabric. "It's beautiful."

"Well, you should definitely wear it for the ceremony," Morty said. "It would look very elegant at the piano."

Clara nodded and carefully re-folded the wrap. She was so happy to have received such a thoughtful gift. It helped her realize that she had a place in this community and that she was making a real contribution to the island itself. She had come to Wisteria Island so broken and alone, looking only for solitude in her grief.

Instead, she'd found connection, purpose, and the slow return of joy. Playing for Danielle and Bennett's wedding felt like a milestone in her healing journey, a real sign that she was ready to participate fully in life again.

"Well, back to business," Morty said, looking at his clipboard again. "The quartet will need to be positioned optimally for sound projection. I was thinking here—about the eastern column of the gazebo, but obviously I will defer to your expertise."

Clara nodded, already visualizing the setup in her mind. "The eastern column would work well, especially with the direction of the breeze at sunset. We'll need to angle the keyboard slightly so I can see the officiant and the couple."

"Brilliant, brilliant," Morty said, scribbling notes. "And we'll have a few reserved chairs nearby for you and the musicians during the non-performance portions of the ceremony. I thought we could use those ivory cushions with the embroidered details, the ones Dorothy found at that antique market."

Clara chuckled. "Only you would remember embroidery details on chair cushions in the middle of a potential music emergency."

"I have layers," he said, pretending to fluff his imaginary collar. "Now, about postlude selections. Are we leaning romantic or triumphant?"

As Morty continued outlining the logistics of the big day, Clara found herself smiling. All the pre-wedding chaos, the musical challenges, and the countless details still had to be finalized, and all of it felt vibrant and alive, a welcome contrast to the numbing fog that had enveloped her for so many months after her husband's death.

Robert would have loved this, she thought. He always thrived on the energy of the preparation and the anticipation before an event. He would have approved of her beautiful new wrap, her contribution to Danielle and Bennett's special day, and most of all, her gradual return to the world of the living.

And for the first time, the thought brought more comfort than pain.

Bennett stood in his office and looked out the window at the flurry of activity going on. The last-minute wedding preparations had taken the normally peaceful island and turned it into a hive of productive energy. It was exciting to see the residents, all of whom were older than 60, enjoying life and being useful. Some of them hadn't felt that in a very long time.

Morty darted from place to place like a frantic hummingbird with his clipboard in hand. He coordinated everything from chair deliveries to flower arrangements, and Bennett had to say that he was very impressed by just how much energy Morty had. He didn't realize it until now. Morty was more spry than most 25-year-olds. He decided they would have to surprise Morty and Dorothy with something special after the wedding. Maybe a day-trip to Seagrove for some antiquing.

Dorothy supervised a team that arranged tables at the community center, and her commanding presence made sure everything was positioned with military precision. Bennett often thought she missed her calling as a drill sergeant rather than having been a Hollywood star.

Even the residents who weren't officially

involved in planning had found ways to contribute. Gladys was baking her famous lemon cookies for the welcome baskets for out-of-town guests. Ted and several others were stringing lights along the paths leading to the gazebo. Esther had even taken over the community center kitchen with a small army of volunteers to prepare the rehearsal dinner.

It was exactly what Bennett had envisioned when he created Wisteria Island - a true community where everybody got to contribute their talents and support each other through all of life's moments.

A knock at the door pulled him from his thoughts.

"Come on in," he called, turning from the window.

Danielle entered, looking slightly frazzled but beautiful as always.

"Ah, there you are. I've been looking everywhere. Did you approve the final menu with Esther? She's asking me something about seafood appetizers."

"All approved," Bennett said, crossing to meet her. "Everything is under control. Breathe."

She laughed and allowed him to pull her into his arms. "I am breathing - mostly. Just enough not to die, I think. It's just there's so much to do, and my mom keeps adding her 'small suggestions' that somehow require major restructuring. Morty nearly had a stroke when the florist called to say that they might be delayed in some traffic on the mainland due to some parade that's happening."

He silenced her with a gentle kiss. When they broke apart, he kept his forehead pressed to hers.

"In three days, we'll be married. All this other stuff is just details."

She exhaled slowly, tension starting to leave her shoulders. "You're right. I know you're right. I just want everything to be perfect, and not even for me or you. I want it to be perfect for them because they've worked so hard."

"It will be perfect because we'll be together, and that's all they really want. Surrounded by the people we love in a place that brought us together, nothing else really matters."

She smiled up at him. "When did you get so wise?"

"I have my moments," he said. "Now, I believe we have a rehearsal dinner seating chart to finalize before Morty and your mother come over here and start giving orders."

"Mom thinks seating should reflect appropriate

social hierarchy, whatever that means, and Morty is insisting on optimal conversational dynamics."

"Well, let's put them all at the same table and let them battle it out in person," Bennett said, winking.

"Oh, don't you tempt me."

Danielle pulled away from him reluctantly. "I gotta get back to the clinic. Dr. Patel is doing final patient reviews before she takes over next week."

"How's that going?"

"Wonderfully, actually. She's compassionate, competent, and the residents really seem to like her. I feel confident leaving the island in her hands while we're away."

She paused at the door. "Which reminds me, you still haven't told me where we're going on our honeymoon."

Bennett smiled. "And I'm not going to. It's a surprise."

"You're impossible," she said, with her hands on her hips.

"And you love it."

"I love you," she corrected, blowing him a kiss before she departed.

Alone again, Bennett returned to the window, his heart full as he watched his island community come together to celebrate the biggest day of his life. In three days, Danielle would be his wife. After years of building Wisteria Island on faith and prayer and creating this home for others, he had finally found his own home in her.

CHAPTER 10

Cecilia surveyed the gazebo with a critical eye, as she did everything. She made some minor adjustments to the draped fabric that would frame the ceremony space. The white gauzy material caught the breeze and billowed gently before it settled again around the columns.

"A bit higher on the left," she directed Janice, who stood on a stepladder making the adjustments. She had called for Eddie, but he was busy with something else, and she didn't have time to wait. Janice claimed she had the best balance on the island - and she did square dance all the time - although Cecilia wasn't sure that had anything at all to do with balance.

"We want it to appear effortless, like the breeze created the perfect folds."

"Effortless," Janice repeated. "Like everything else about this wedding."

Cecilia smiled despite herself. She'd come to appreciate the dry humor and spirit of Wisteria's residents over the past weeks. Their dedication to making Danielle and Bennett's wedding special touched her deeply, even if their methods sometimes lacked the polished precision she was accustomed to in New York event planning.

"Perfect," she said when Janice finished the adjustment. "Now, do you have the blue ribbon for tomorrow's final decoration?"

"All ready," Janice said, climbing down from the ladder. "Dorothy's keeping it in her cottage to prevent any mishaps. You know how Morty gets when he's excited. He's like a tornado in human form."

Cecilia laughed, picturing Morty's enthusiastic but occasionally chaotic assistance. "He means well."

"Well, they all do," came a voice from behind them.

Danielle approached, looking pretty in her simple sundress with her hair twisted up.

"Dear, I thought you were at the clinic," Cecilia said, kissing her daughter on the cheek.

"I just finished. Dr. Patel has everything well in hand." She looked at the finished gazebo. "Mom, it looks beautiful. You've transformed this place into something magical."

Cecilia felt an unexpected surge of emotion. "You know I wanted it to be perfect for you."

"And it is," Danielle said, hugging her impulsively.

Janice tactfully gathered her supplies. "I'm just going to take these back to the community center. Morty's doing a final review of the table settings."

Janice walked off as Danielle and Cecilia stood together in the gazebo, the ocean breeze gently dancing with the draped fabric.

"You know," Danielle said, "when I first told you I wanted my wedding here, I never imagined you would do all of this. I thought we'd just set up a few chairs on the beach and that would be that, and then you'd go back to New York City and nothing would change."

"Well, that would have been charming, I suppose, in its own way. But some occasions deserve proper recognition."

"Is that why you and Dad never renewed your

vows or had big anniversary celebrations? Because your original wedding wasn't proper in your eyes?"

"Well, perhaps. But your father and I had our own issues, though he always said our courthouse wedding was perfect precisely because it was about us and there were no distractions. And he claimed the best wedding gift was not having to remember which fork to use at a formal reception."

Danielle laughed. "That sounds just like Dad."

"Oh, but he would have loved this, you know," Cecilia said. "Not necessarily the event itself, but what it represents. You finding your place, your person, and your purpose all at the same time."

"I wish he could be here," Danielle said.

"And I do too, for your benefit." Cecilia reached for her daughter's hand. "I can say confidently that he would be so proud of you and of the choices you've made and the life you've built."

"Even though they weren't the choices you wanted for me?"

Cecilia sighed. "I wanted success and security for you, and I thought I knew exactly what that should look like. But seeing you here with Bennett and your community, I know now that you found something I didn't even know to wish for you. And it comes along with its own success and security."

"Thank you for saying that," Danielle said.

"I should have said it long ago, but I'm not particularly good at expressing… you know… feelings." Cecilia scrunched her nose as if the word was foreign to her. "It's a professional hazard. Science demands objectivity."

"You're not just a scientist, Mom. You're also a person. A mother. A woman."

"I know. And I'm trying to be a better one of all of those." She reached into her pocket and pulled out a small velvet pouch. "I have something else for you. Not your something blue - we're saving that for the ceremony. This is just something I thought you might like to have."

Danielle accepted the pouch and carefully opened it, tipping the contents into her palm. A delicate gold locket gleamed in the sunlight.

"That was your grandmother's," Cecilia said. "My mother wore it on her wedding day, and I wore it on mine."

She opened the locket to find two tiny photographs—one of her parents on their wedding day and one of her grandparents.

"I thought perhaps we might add a picture of you and Bennett. A sort of family tradition, if you'd like."

Danielle closed her hand around the locket. "I would love that, Mom. Thank you."

They stood together, looking at the ocean view framed by the gazebo's elegant columns. Three generations of women, their marriages, their lives, all connected by the simple gold locket.

"Now then," Cecilia said, moving back to practicality, "we should check on the final flower delivery. The orchids from Charleston are due this afternoon, and Dorothy's convinced they need her personal inspection before we can arrange them."

They walked back toward the center of the island, arm in arm, Danielle realizing that the past weeks had brought the most unexpected gift. Not just a beautiful wedding, but a new understanding with her mother.

Their relationship wasn't perfect. No mother-daughter relationship is perfect. And there would probably still be moments of friction and misunderstanding. But they'd built a bridge where there had once only been distance.

Another gift from Wisteria Island.

CHAPTER 11

B ennett found Danielle on their deck late in the evening, staring at the ocean with a troubled expression on her face. The rehearsal dinner was tomorrow night, and the wedding was just a couple of days away, but he sensed there was worry in her shoulders.

"Everything okay?" he asked.

She leaned against him, welcoming his arm around her waist. "I'm worried about my mom."

"Wedding jitters? Second thoughts on the orchid arrangements?" he said, attempting to joke, but she didn't smile.

"Her blood pressure is still up," she said. "I've been monitoring it every day, and the medication just isn't bringing it down as much as I'd hoped.

She's still having the headaches, and this afternoon, I swear I saw her hands trembling a little bit."

He frowned. "Well, that does sound concerning. Has she seen anybody besides you?"

"You know my mom. She will insist on waiting until after the wedding for any 'unnecessary medical drama,' as she puts it. I tried calling her regular doctor in New York, but she wouldn't authorize a release of the records to me."

"What's your medical opinion? Not as her daughter, but as her nurse."

She hesitated. "Well, without a full workup, I just can't be certain. But I'm worried about the exhaustion compounded by the high blood pressure. She's been pushing herself way too hard with the wedding planning, barely sleeping, probably not taking her medication consistently."

"Is this dangerous?"

"Well, it could be if it was left untreated. I mean, she needs rest, proper medication, and monitoring. I'm worried she might just collapse if she keeps up this pace."

"What can we do? I mean, if she's refusing further treatment until after the wedding."

"That's just it. I don't know." She turned to face him. "Part of me wants to scale everything back, you know, make the wedding so simple she can't do anything to oversee another detail. But another part knows that she would never forgive me if I changed all these plans because of her health. She's just determined to make everything perfect."

"Well, what if we enlisted help? Dorothy and Morty could take over more of the coordination. We could tell them your mother needs to delegate for medical reasons."

"Maybe," Danielle said. "Perhaps I could adjust her medication dosage, perhaps add something mild to help her sleep."

"I could also speak with her," Bennett offered. "I mean, not about her health, but about how much we appreciate what she's done and how any remaining details are well in hand. Just give her permission to step back without feeling like she's failing us."

Danielle smiled. "That might work. I mean, she respects you. She's less likely to dismiss your concerns as overprotectiveness the way she does with me."

"Well, consider it done," he promised. "We'll find a way to get her to slow down without making her feel like she's being sidelined. And after the wedding, she will get proper medical care."

"Thank you." Danielle leaned in and kissed him

softly. "I know it's a lot to handle right before our wedding."

"Hey, this is what a partnership looks like. Remember, your concerns are my concerns, especially when it comes to our family."

They stood together watching moonlight on the water, and Bennett made a silent vow to always make Danielle's concerns his concerns, no matter what they were.

Three empty coffee cups sat on the deck railing of Morty's cottage. It was early, but the mission was important. Dorothy adjusted her wide-brimmed hat against the morning sun, and Clara reviewed her checklist for the third time.

"Remind me again why we had to meet at six o'clock in the morning," Dorothy said, stifling a yawn behind her recently manicured hand.

"Well, because the rehearsal dinner is tonight," Morty said with exaggerated patience. "That means today's our last chance to make sure everything's perfectly in place for tomorrow's ceremony. We have to complete our inspection before Danielle and Bennett notice what we're doing."

"Oh yes, heaven forbid the bride and groom should know that we're ensuring their wedding goes smoothly," Dorothy drawled. "That's such a terrible surprise."

"It's not about surprising them," Clara said. "It's about allowing them to focus on each other rather than all the details of the wedding. Today and tomorrow should be about their relationship, not whether the chair ribbons are evenly distributed."

Dorothy tilted her head. "Very well, what's first on this military operations list of yours, General Morty?"

Morty looked at his clipboard, which he'd been clutching since dawn. "Clara will verify that the musical instruments have been properly positioned and tuned at the community center before the reception. Then she'll meet with the string quartet when they arrive at 11. Dorothy, I need you to supervise the final placement of the orchids at the gazebo. They were delivered last night, and they're being kept cool in the kitchen refrigerators."

"And you?" Dorothy asked.

"I'm confirming all transportation arrangements for our off-island guests. The last thing we need is Danielle's former hospital colleagues stranded on the mainland because they missed the special ferry."

Clara smiled at how serious Morty was. His dedication to ensuring the perfect day for Danielle and Bennett was touching—if occasionally overwhelming in its intensity. Over the past few weeks, she'd come to the understanding that his over-the-top enthusiasm was his way of showing love. The more color schemes and sequins, the deeper his affection was.

Morty nodded. "Now we need to split up. Remember, stealth and efficiency." He tapped his watch dramatically. "Meet back here at noon for a progress update."

As they went on their way for their respective missions, Clara couldn't help but smile at this unlikely friendship she had developed with a flamboyant, fashionable man, a glamorous former movie star, and herself, a widowed conductor.

Wisteria Island just had a way of bringing people together who might never have connected elsewhere.

Clara's assignment took her to the community center, which had been transformed for tomorrow's reception. The large open space had tables dotted all around it, each set with crisp white linens and simple but beautiful centerpieces using orchids and sea glass. Tiny little lights had been strung overhead, creating the effect of a starlit sky.

Clara couldn't believe how beautiful the community center looked.

The grand piano, rented from Savannah and delivered at a considerable expense, stood on a small raised platform in the corner. She ran her fingers over the keys, playing a quick scale to check the tuning. Perfect. Although she would play the keyboard at the wedding site near the gazebo, she would play this beautiful piano during the reception. Bennett had spared no expense to make sure the music would be exceptional.

She worked through her checklist, making sure that everything was as it should be, and felt a familiar presence—not a ghostly one, but the comforting sense that her husband would have approved of her involvement in all of this and of her return to music. He would also approve of her new friendships, and for the first time since his death, she could think of him with more joy than pain, remembering instead his passion for bringing people together through music, rather than focusing on the absence of him.

Tomorrow, she would play for a wedding, a celebration of love and commitment that might have been unbearably painful to witness at one point, just a few weeks ago. Now, even though she still felt nostalgic for her husband, it felt perfectly right to contribute to Danielle and Bennett's special day.

Her music would be her gift to them, and in a way, their love was a gift to her—a reminder that life continues on, that joy returns eventually, and that new chapters begin even when beloved stories end.

The morning of the rehearsal dinner dawned beautiful and clear, with a slight breeze that carried the scent of sea and flowers across the whole island. Everything was ready. The gazebo was decorated, the community center was transformed, and the last details were perfectly in place for the ceremony tomorrow.

Danielle had just finished her morning rounds at the clinic when Dorothy suddenly burst through the door, very flustered, which was quite uncharacteristic for her.

"Your mother," she said. "She's having some sort of episode at the gazebo. She asked me to find you."

Danielle's heart pounded. "What kind of episode?"

"She became very dizzy while we were finalizing the flower arrangements. Had to sit down rather suddenly. She's saying it's nothing, of course, but her color is off and she's not making her usual commentary about my decorative choices."

Danielle grabbed her medical bag. "I'll go right now. Could you find Bennett and ask him to meet me there?"

By the time Danielle reached the gazebo, her mom was seated on one of the benches, looking pale. Morty was hovering nearby, offering glasses of water, but Cecilia waved him away impatiently.

"This is entirely unnecessary," she said as Danielle approached. "I just stood up too fast after adjusting the orchid arrangement."

"Okay, well humor me," Danielle said, already taking out her blood pressure cuff. "Let's just check your numbers."

Cecilia submitted, extending her arm while Morty gave her a pointed look.

"Don't you have a ribbon arrangement to oversee?" she said to him.

"Ribbons can wait," he replied firmly. "Some things are more important than decoration."

Danielle wrapped the cuff around her mother's arm and took the reading.

"175 over 100." Higher than yesterday, despite her medication. Her concern grew.

"Mom, your blood pressure is still climbing. Don't tell me it's just because you're annoyed with all of us. These numbers have been trending upwards for days."

"I might have forgotten a dose or two," Cecilia said reluctantly. "This planning has been rather all-consuming."

Before Danielle could respond, Bennett arrived. He looked calm but concerned.

"Cecilia," he said, sitting beside her on the bench, "I think we might need to make some adjustments to today's schedule."

"I'm perfectly capable," she started.

"Of course you are," Bennett interrupted. "That's never been a question. But Danielle and I have been talking, and we realize we've been so unfair to you."

She blinked in surprise. "What? Unfair? How?"

"Well, we've allowed you to shoulder so much of the wedding preparation burden. You've been working non-stop, and we've been so caught up in our own excitement that we haven't properly acknowledged everything you've done."

"Well, that's what mothers do," Cecilia said.

"Perhaps. But you deserve to enjoy the celebration too, and not just work yourself through it. So here's what we propose. Dorothy and Morty are going to take over the final coordination duties for today and tomorrow. Of course, you'll still be consulted on any major decisions, but all the hands-on work will be theirs and whoever they get to help them."

"Absolutely," Dorothy agreed. "I've directed enough film sets to handle a wedding coordination."

"And I've been taking meticulous notes of all your specifications," Morty said. "Every ribbon placement, every floral arrangement, all according to your standards."

Cecilia looked at all of them suspiciously. "You know, this feels like a conspiracy."

"No, Mom, it's us recognizing you," Danielle said, "for how much you've done and how much we just want you to be able to enjoy the results of your hard work." She took her mother's hand. "Please, let us do this for you."

Cecilia's expression softened. Maybe she was just too exhausted to maintain her usual level of control.

"Well, I suppose I could use a bit of rest before tonight's rehearsal dinner."

"Great," Bennett said, offering his hand to help her up. "I'm going to walk you back to your cottage.

Danielle's going to finish her morning appointments. Dorothy and Morty are eager to prove their coordinating capabilities."

As they walked slowly along the path leading to Cecilia's cottage, she sighed. "This is about my blood pressure, isn't it?"

"Well, it's about wanting my future mother-in-law to be well enough to dance at our wedding," Bennett said. "And yeah, Danielle is very concerned about your health. We both are."

"I never wanted to cause anyone worry," she said. "I just wanted everything to be perfect for Danielle. She deserves that."

"She also deserves to have her mother healthy and present. Above all else," he said gently. "Those details at the wedding matter far less than you do."

They walked in silence for a moment before Cecilia spoke again. "You know, I missed so many important moments in her life because of my career. I missed school plays, sports competitions, even her college graduation. There was always some conference or research deadline that took precedence." She shook her head. "I don't want to miss this, too."

"You won't. But you need to rest today, take your medication properly, and let everybody else handle the details." He smiled. "I promise we won't let Morty add sequins to the gazebo columns while you're napping."

That earned a small laugh. "Very well. I'll be the perfect patient for the remainder of the day."

As they reached her cottage, she looked at him. "You know, you're good for her. I wasn't entirely convinced at first, but I am now."

"Thank you," he said. "That means a great deal coming from you."

"Take care of her," she said, "even when she insists she doesn't need it. She can be a bit like her mother."

"I will," he promised. "Now you go rest - nurse's orders."

As he watched Cecilia enter her cottage, he sent a quick text to Danielle:

> Mission accomplished. Your mother has agreed to rest and let Dorothy and Morty handle the remaining details. Coming back to check on you.

The crisis had been averted for now, but he had no illusions that Cecilia was going to let other people control all the wedding preparations. He just hoped this intervention would ensure she made it through the celebrations without a serious health incident. Danielle always reminded him that the best medical treatment was prevention. In this case, they were trying to prevent Cecilia Wright from working herself into collapse.

The rehearsal dinner was in full swing at Esther's Restaurant, which had been closed to the public for this private event, although most of the island was in attendance. Long tables had been arranged on the deck overlooking the water, decorated with hurricane lamps and simple arrangements of beach roses and sea lavender. Bennett stood at the head of one of the tables, looking at the scene with quiet satisfaction.

Danielle sat beside him, radiant, wearing a simple pale blue dress and laughing at something Morty had said. Cecilia was deep in conversation with Dr. Patel, probably something about viruses, while Dorothy regaled several mainland guests with what was undoubtedly one of her highly embellished Hollywood anecdotes. Around the other tables, island residents mingled with a few of the off-island guests, Danielle's former colleagues from New York, Bennett's business associates who had become friends over the years, and Cecilia's fellow researchers. The blending of the worlds felt right and natural.

"Penny for your thoughts," came a voice at his elbow.

Clara appeared beside him, elegant, wearing a silver-gray shimmery dress with the blue silk wrap he and Danielle had given her.

"I'm just standing here counting my blessings," Bennett said. "You know, a year ago I never would have imagined all of this."

She nodded. "Well, life has a way of surprising us, sometimes painfully and sometimes wonderfully."

"And sometimes both at the same time," Bennett said. "If Danielle hadn't been hurt by her ex, she never would have come to the island."

"And if I hadn't lost Robert, I wouldn't be here either," she said. "Not that I wouldn't trade all of this to have him back for even one day, but there's a certain grace in finding meaning after loss."

"There is," Bennett agreed. "You know, my grand-mother used to say that joy and sorrow are two sides of the same coin. You truly can't appreciate one without ever having known the other."

"Sounds like a very wise woman."

"Oh, she was. I think she and Robert would have gotten along great."

Clara smiled. "Probably just comparing notes on how to manage headstrong grandchildren and spouses."

"Exactly," Bennett laughed. "Speaking of headstrong, I should probably rescue Danielle from Morty's last-minute wedding suggestions. I believe he's now advocating for releasing butterflies during our vows."

"Doves, actually," Clara said, scrunching her nose. "The butterflies were deemed, quote, too unpredictable in their flight patterns."

Bennett rolled his eyes. "Heaven forbid that we have unpredictable butterflies at our wedding."

He walked back over to rejoin Danielle, and Eddie appeared at his side, looking uncharacteristically formal, wearing a pressed shirt and tie, although the tie was about five inches too short and his buttons were pulling as if any one of them would give at any moment.

"Hey, boss. A special delivery has arrived. It's in your office, as you requested."

"Perfect timing. Thanks, Eddie."

Bennett made his way to Danielle, bending over to whisper in her ear. "Would you mind stepping away for a minute? I just have something I need to show you."

Her eyebrows raised. "Now? In the middle of dinner?"

"Trust me," he said, offering his hand.

They slipped away unnoticed because Morty had launched into a toast that promised to be both lengthy and extravagant. He captured everyone's attention with his theatrical gestures as Bennett led Danielle out the door and along the moonlit path toward his office.

"Where are we going?" she asked, their fingers intertwined. "And why do you look so mysteriously pleased with yourself?"

"You need to have patience, Miss Wright," he said. "All will be revealed."

When they reached his office, Bennett paused with his hand on the doorknob.

"Now, close your eyes," he said.

She raised an eyebrow but complied. He guided her inside and put her in the center of the room.

"Okay, open them."

Danielle did and gasped.

Sitting on Bennett's desk was a beautiful wooden music box, its polished surface inlaid with mother-of-pearl in an intricate pattern of wisteria blossoms.

"Oh, Bennett," she said, "it's beautiful." She walked closer to examine it.

"Open it."

She carefully lifted the lid. Inside, the small mechanism started to turn and the notes of Pachelbel's Canon filled the room. The same music that would play tomorrow as she walked down the aisle toward him.

"I had it custom-made. Clara helped me with the musical arrangement."

She traced the inlaid flowers with her fingertip. "It is absolutely incredible. I can't believe you thought of this."

"There's more. Look inside the lid," he said.

Danielle tilted the box to catch the light and saw an engraving:

For my Danielle,
Love is not found but built.
One day, one moment, one note at a time.
All my love, always,
Bennett

Tears welled up in her eyes. "Oh, Bennett."

"I wanted to give you something that would remind you of our beginning. You know, something that captures what Wisteria Island means to us. Its beauty, the music, building something lasting together."

She set the music box carefully on the desk and threw her arms around his neck.

"It's perfect. And you're perfect."

She kissed him deeply, pouring all of her love into the embrace.

When they finally broke apart, he rested his forehead against hers.

"One more day. Tomorrow, you'll be my wife."

"I can't wait," Danielle whispered back.

CHAPTER 12

The night before her wedding, Danielle couldn't sleep. Her beautiful dress hung on the back of her bedroom door. Her something blue bracelet sat in its velvet box on the dresser, and Bennett's beautiful music box played softly from the nightstand. Everything was ready, but sleep remained elusive. Her mind was way too full of anticipation to shut off for the evening.

She finally gave up and slipped on a light robe before stepping out onto the deck of her cottage, sitting in a comfortable chair Bennett had built for her when he renovated the cottage after the hurricane. The night was clear. Stars scattered across a velvet sky, their light reflecting on the calm surface of the water. In the distance, she could just make out the silhouette of the gazebo, where tomorrow she would become Bennett's wife.

The thought of this brought a grin to her lips. After years of focusing on her career and protecting herself from vulnerability after her ex's betrayal, she found love in the most unexpected place, a small retirement island that had become home in every sense of the word. She had so many grandpas and grandmas on the island that it was hard to keep up with her new family tree.

A soft knock at the door interrupted her thoughts. She had no idea who would be visiting her at this late hour, but when she went to answer it, she found her mother standing on the porch.

"Mom, is everything okay?"

"Oh, of course," Cecilia replied, smoothing her silk robe. "I just saw your light was on and thought, well, I remember the night before my wedding. I couldn't sleep a wink. My mom came to sit with me." She shrugged slightly. "Maybe it's a silly tradition, but I thought…"

"Maybe I'd love some company?" Danielle said, stepping aside and allowing her mom to enter. "I was gonna make some chamomile tea. Would you like some?"

"Oh, that would be lovely."

They settled on the deck with their steaming mugs of tea, the night air cool but not too uncomfortable. They sat in silence for a while, just watching the stars and listening to the waves.

"You know, your grandmother was terrified I'd back out," Cecilia said. "That's why she came to sit with me, just to make sure I didn't flee in the night." She smiled. "As if I would have. I loved your father from the moment he questioned my research methodology at that conference."

Danielle laughed. "Only you would find criticism romantic, Mom."

"Well, it wasn't really criticism. He was trying to engage with me. It showed me that he took my work seriously, and at that time, a lot of men didn't. Howard always took everything I cared about seriously, whether he shared the interest or not. I think that's rare."

"Yeah, Bennett's that way, too," Danielle said. "He listens. I mean, really listens, even when I'm just rambling on about a difficult patient or some crazy medical journal article."

"That's how I know he's right for you," Cecilia said. She sipped her tea. "I wasn't sure at first, you know, not because of any failing on his part, but because this life..." She gestured toward the island. "I mean, it's so different from what I envisioned for you."

"I know."

"But seeing you here and watching how you've just flourished…" She reached over and took Danielle's hand. "Well, you were right to follow your heart. I'm sorry if I made that more difficult than it needed to be."

Danielle squeezed her mother's hand. "Thanks for saying that. And thank you for embracing and including yourself in our wedding plans to help make tomorrow so special."

"It's been my pleasure. However, I draw the line at Morty's last-minute dove suggestion. Some things are simply a step too far."

They both laughed. Danielle realized that this was perhaps one of the first times she and her mom had truly laughed together as adults, not just polite chuckles at a formal dinner. Another gift of Wisteria Island, she thought.

"You should try to get some sleep," Cecilia said. "A bride needs rest, because you certainly don't want dark circles under your eyes tomorrow."

Danielle stood as well, hugging her mother. "Thank you for coming over. It means a lot to me."

"I love you, Danielle," she said quietly as she

hugged her. "And I'm so proud of the woman you've become."

As her mother left, Danielle returned to her bedroom, surprised to find herself feeling drowsy. She settled under the covers, played the music box again, and closed her eyes.

Tomorrow, she would marry Bennett. She would begin her life with the man of her dreams, surrounded by the unlikely band of misfits that was their Wisteria Island family. It would be the beginning of a new chapter.

And with that peaceful thought, she drifted into sleep, dreaming of white gazebos, ocean breezes, and the handsome man who would soon become her husband.

The morning of Danielle and Bennett's wedding was clear and perfect, with the most beautiful blue sky. It was as if Wisteria Island itself was celebrating with them. A gentle breeze kept the humidity at bay, and there was not a hint of a cloud in the sky.

Clara woke up before sunrise, unable to keep a mixture of excitement and responsibility from breaking her slumber. Today, her music would shape one of the most important moments in Danielle and Bennett's lives. It was a little bit intimidating, but very gratifying. She dressed carefully in a simple but elegant navy dress, arranging her silver hair in a neat twist. The beautiful blue wrap they'd given her would complete the outfit for the ceremony.

She checked the clock and saw it was still quite early, just past seven. The wedding wasn't until four in the afternoon, but there was just so much to do before then. She had scheduled a final rehearsal with the string quartet at nine, followed by a sound check at the gazebo. She would serve as the musical director for the day, and she wanted everything to be perfect. Not just technically perfect, although that mattered a lot, but emotionally resonant with everybody there. Music had the power to elevate a ceremony from just being lovely to being transcendent. She wanted to give Danielle and Bennett nothing less than her best.

A knock at the door interrupted her thoughts. She opened it and found Morty on her doorstep, already dressed in his wedding finery, even though it was way too early for that. He wore a lavender suit with a bow tie patterned in shades of seafoam green and purple.

"Good morning, maestro," he greeted her with his typical enthusiasm. "I come bearing sustenance for the artist." He held out a white basket with a thermos, muffins, and fruit.

"Oh, Morty, how thoughtful. Come in," Clara said. She accepted the basket. "Though I must say, you're beautifully dressed rather early. I mean, this ceremony isn't for nine hours."

He straightened his bow tie. "A fashion statement of this magnitude requires time to achieve its full impact," he said, turning around in a circle. "Besides, there are a thousand details to oversee. No rest for the wedding planner extraordinaire," he said, raising his arm in the air.

Clara laughed, pouring coffee from the thermos into two mugs. "How are Danielle and Bennett this morning? Have you seen them?"

"Oh, Bennett is as cool as a cucumber, as usual. Helping Eddie with some last-minute adjustments to the gazebo lighting. Danielle, on the other hand," he said dramatically, "well, is experiencing what I believe professionals would call pre-wedding jitters."

"Oh, dear, is it serious?"

"Oh, nothing that won't be cured the moment she sees Bennett waiting at the gazebo," he said. "Her mother's with her now, which seems to be helping a bit. They've become quite close these past few weeks. It's rather touching."

Clara nodded. "And the gazebo decorations, all according to plan?"

"Absolute perfection," Morty said. "The orchids are magnificent. Every bloom positioned precisely according to Dorothy's standards. The fabric draping has never looked more elegant, and the ribbons add just the right touch of color."

They continued chatting while finishing their coffee as Morty ran through his extensive checklist, and Clara continued to offer calm reassurance. Even though Morty was very theatrical, Clara had come to appreciate his meticulous attention to detail and his earnest desire to make the day so special for the couple.

"You know, I should go check on the quartet," Clara said. "They were supposed to get here early."

"Oh, and I need to consult with Cecilia about the processional timing," Morty said. "Oh, and I almost forgot." He reached into an inner pocket of his suit and produced a small envelope. "Bennett asked me to give you this."

Clara took it curiously, opening it after Morty walked away. Inside was a simple note written in Bennett's precise handwriting.

Dear Clara,

I want to thank you for sharing your gift of music with us today. It's going to make our ceremony complete, and your friendship has meant more to Danielle and me than we can express. The gazebo will remain on Wisteria Island long after today's celebration, and it will be a permanent addition to the lives of the residents on the island. We've decided to name it Whitman Gazebo in honor of you and Robert. May it be a place where music and memory continue to bring joy to our community for years to come.

With our deepest gratitude,

Bennett

Clara sat perfectly still, the note trembling slightly in her hand. This unexpected tribute to her husband, to both of them, touched her deeply. That their names would forever be linked to a place that had such beauty and meaning felt like the perfect memorial. For so long after his death, Clara had focused on what was lost. Coming to Wisteria

Island, she had slowly and painfully started to realize what remained. The music they had shared, the love that continued in his absence, and the ability to form new connections while honoring what had come before.

The Whitman Gazebo, a place of music and memory, of celebration and quiet contemplation. Robert would have loved it.

With renewed purpose, Clara gathered her musical papers and headed out to meet the quartet. Today was a day for joy and new beginnings.

Danielle stood in her bedroom and watched as Dorothy carefully arranged the delicate flowers in her hair. Her beautiful wedding dress hung perfectly against her skin, its simple elegance exactly what she had envisioned for herself.

"Hold still, darling," Dorothy instructed, putting in another flower with a pearl-tipped pin. "You know, beauty requires lots of patience."

"And a steady hand," Morty added, as he hovered nearby with his emergency sewing kit. "Thankfully, Dorothy possesses that in abundance. Unlike some people I could mention," he looked at himself in the reflection of the mirror, where his lavender bow tie sat slightly askew, despite multiple attempts to straighten it.

"Has anybody checked in on my mother this morning?" Danielle asked. The memory of her episode remained vivid in her mind.

"I brought her breakfast myself," Morty said. "She's already dressed in her stunning rose ensemble and looks remarkably well-rested. She even asked me to tell you that she's taking her medication like a model patient."

"Her color was much improved," Dorothy added, "and she wasn't even trying to micromanage the floral arrangements when I stopped by, which I consider a miracle in and of itself."

Danielle smiled, feeling some of the tension leave her shoulders. "Thank you both so much. I couldn't help worrying after yesterday."

"Well, that's perfectly understandable," Dorothy said as she secured the final flower. "But today is for joy, not worry. Your mother's a strong woman. A little high blood pressure isn't going to keep her from her only daughter's wedding."

Morty walked over with a small velvet box. "Speaking of your mother, she asked me to bring this to you and said you'd know what it was."

Danielle opened the box to find the gold locket, the one that had belonged to her grandmother, that her own mother had worn on her wedding day. A note tucked inside read simply, *For the newest bride in our family. Your father would be so proud. Love, Mom.*

"Oh," Danielle breathed, feeling tears threatening to spill over and ruin her newly applied makeup.

"None of that!" Morty yelled, gently taking the locket and fastening it around her neck. "We've spent far too long on your makeup for tears, my dear."

Dorothy handed her a tissue. "Blot, don't wipe," she instructed. "And maybe this is a moment for some traditional wedding day wisdom."

"From the woman who's been married four times?" Morty teased.

Dorothy gave him a look. "Which makes me an expert. I've learned what works and what doesn't."

Danielle laughed. "I'll take wisdom from wherever it comes today."

Dorothy took her hands, suddenly serious. "Marriage is a dance, darling. Sometimes you lead, sometimes you follow. But you must always remain in step with each other. Bennett is a wonderful man who adores you. But even good men need guidance occasionally."

"And patience," Morty added. He turned to Danielle. "You know, the best advice I can give you, my dear, is to simply remember why you fell in love with Bennett in the first place. In the day-to-day of your marriage, it'll be easy to forget the magic of all these early moments. But keep them close to your heart, especially when you have disagreements about which way the toilet paper should hang."

"Well, it's over the top, obviously," Dorothy said.

"Under is clearly superior for decorative folding purposes," Morty said.

Danielle laughed. "So this is your sage marriage advice? Toilet paper orientation?"

"Oh, you'd be surprised at how many arguments come from such trivial matters," Dorothy said. "But you know, the real advice is to build traditions together. Little rituals that are uniquely yours. Well, Gordon and I—he was husband number two, the good one—we had breakfast in bed every Sunday, rain or shine, for 23 years. Even when we were fighting about something else, we always had those Sunday mornings."

"Bennett and I watch the sunrise together when we can," Danielle said. "You know, just coffee and quiet to begin our days."

"Perfect," Morty said. "You hold on to that. Add

new traditions as you go. Maybe a sunset walk when you're eighty, complaining about your arthritis while holding hands."

A knock at the door interrupted them, and Clara peeked in. "It's almost time," she said. "Bennett is already at the gazebo and looks terribly handsome and very nervous." Her eyes widened when she looked at Danielle. "Oh my goodness, you look absolutely beautiful."

"And the final touch," Dorothy declared, carefully placing a simple veil that attached at the crown of Danielle's head, framing the flowers in her hair. "There, perfect."

Danielle turned to the mirror, barely recognizing the woman gazing back at her. The simple elegance of the dress, the fresh flowers in her hair, and the gold locket catching the light coming through the window—they had all transformed her into a bride. But more importantly, into a woman ready to begin this new chapter of her life.

"Thank you all," she said, turning to hug each of her friends. "For everything. Not just today, but for welcoming me to this island, becoming my family, and helping me find my way to this moment."

"Oh, stop," Morty said, waving his hand as his eyes watered. "You have us all in tears, and I've only just perfected the powder I put on my face so I wouldn't shine in the Lowcountry sun."

"Well, it's time to find our seats," Dorothy said. She hugged Danielle one last time before walking to the door.

Morty squeezed her hand. "Now you remember to breathe," he whispered, "and when you see Bennett waiting for you, you forget everything else. Just walk toward your future."

"You do remember you're walking me down the aisle, don't you?" she asked, laughing.

"Oh, honey, I'd never forget that! I get to be the center of attention for a good thirty seconds, walking next to the most beautiful bride in the world."

Danielle stood in her cottage bedroom and stared at herself in the full-length mirror. Her silk dress flowed gracefully from its simple bodice to the floor and caught the light with every movement. Her hair was arranged in loose waves and had tiny white flowers instead of a veil. Around her wrist gleamed her something blue, the sapphire bracelet that had been her father's gift to her mother.

"You look absolutely gorgeous," Cecilia said softly from the doorway. "I've never seen a more stunning bride."

Danielle turned to find her mother watching her with uncharacteristic emotion. Cecilia had chosen a dress in a soft shade of rose rather than her normal neutral colors. The color softened her features and made her look younger, but Danielle was never going to tell her that.

"Thanks, Mom. You look beautiful, too."

Cecilia entered the room and adjusted the delicate gold locket around Danielle's neck.

"I'm so glad I got to be here today."

"How are you feeling?" Danielle asked, worry etched onto her face.

Cecilia smiled. "I'm fine. I promise. Today is your day. Don't worry about me. So, are you ready? Morty says it's time to leave for the gazebo."

Danielle took a deep breath. "I am. I'm just a little bit nervous."

"Well, that's perfectly normal," Cecilia said. "I nearly fainted before walking into that courthouse to marry your father." She smiled at the memory. "But I knew the moment I saw him waiting for me that everything else was going to be okay."

Morty popped his head into the room. "The golf

carts are ready," he said, checking his watch. "Right on schedule."

Though the gazebo was within walking distance, they had arranged for the golf carts to be decorated to match the wedding and transport the wedding party. It was the most glamour they were going to get since they couldn't bring a limousine over to the island. "A bride deserves a proper entrance," Dorothy had declared, and no one had argued with her.

As they got ready to leave, Danielle felt a calm settle over her. The nervous flutter in her stomach turned into something more like peaceful anticipation. In less than an hour, she would be Bennett's wife. The thought filled her with joy.

The drive to the gazebo took them along the island's winding paths, past cottages decorated in ribbons and flowers in honor of their occasion. Residents who weren't even attending the ceremony—although there were few—stood in their yards waving as the small procession passed.

When they reached the bluff overlooking the cove, Danielle caught a glimpse of the wedding site. It looked like a vision against the blue sky and even bluer water, draped with gauzy fabric that billowed in the breeze. White chairs had been arranged in a semicircle facing the ocean view, and they were already filled with guests.

And there, standing at the entrance of the gazebo, was Morty, her chosen escort in her father's absence. He'd slipped away after delivering them to the staging area and changed into a more subdued navy suit for his official role, but she was sure he would change back into the purple one before too much longer.

"Are you ready, my dear?" he asked, offering his arm.

Danielle nodded, took a final moment to smooth her dress, and thought about what was going to happen. This was it—the beginning of her forever with Bennett.

Clara began playing along with the string quartet, and Danielle couldn't help but smile. With Morty at her side, she began to walk toward the gazebo, toward Bennett, and toward their future together.

Bennett stood in the center of the gazebo and tried to maintain his composure as the music started. Eddie stood beside him as his best man and offered silent support as they watched Danielle's mother being escorted to her seat in the front row. The music shifted, signaling the bride's approach, and Bennett's heart felt like it was going to stop.

He saw Danielle appear at the end of the aisle, radiant in her beautiful wedding gown, her smile so big that he could see it from far away. Everyone else disappeared in that moment. There were no guests or decorations, or even a beautiful view. Everything was insignificant compared to Danielle walking toward him.

As she reached the gazebo steps, Morty placed her hand in Bennett's with uncharacteristic seriousness.

"Take care of our girl," he said quietly.

"Always," Bennett said.

Together, they turned to face the pastor. Before he began, Clara's music swelled in a brief interlude, and then they took a moment of reflection and remembrance for those who couldn't be there, like Bennett's grandmother, Danielle's father, and Clara's beloved husband, as well as many other people on the island who had lost those they loved.

Then Bennett and Danielle exchanged vows that they had written for each other.

"Danielle," Bennett started, his voice steady despite the fact that he wanted to break down, "before you came to Wisteria Island, I'd created a community for everyone else, but I remained isolated. You changed all of that, showing me that real connection means being vulnerable, being authentic, and being fully present with another person. I promise you that I'll spend the rest of my life trying to bring you joy every day, trying to understand you, and being the unwavering support that you need. I promise to build our life together with the same care and attention to detail that I gave this island and that you give your patients. I promise to love you through all seasons, all challenges, and all of the unexpected twists and turns our journey may take."

Danielle's eyes watered as she spoke her own vows.

"Bennett, you found me at my lowest point, wounded, disillusioned, and convinced I didn't need anyone. With patience and steady kindness, you showed me what a real partnership would look like. It's not perfect, and it's not without challenges, but it's built on mutual respect and care and love. I promise to be your partner in everything, to support you in your dreams as you've supported mine, and to create a home with you that's filled with laughter. I promise to face whatever life brings us together as a team, and to continue growing with you, learning with you, and building a life - our lives together - one day, one moment, and one memory at a time. I promise to love you completely, honestly, and with my whole heart today and for every day that follows."

They exchanged rings, simple platinum bands that symbolized their lifelong commitment, and then the pastor pronounced them husband and wife as Clara played again, a joyful melody that seemed to fit the mood. Their first kiss as a married couple was met with enthusiastic applause from their island friends and their mainland guests. Cecilia was dabbing discreetly at her eyes in the front row.

As they turned to face all of their guests, now officially Mr. and Mrs. Alexander, Bennett squeezed her hand.

"Happy?" he whispered.

She looked at him, smiling completely. "And you?"

"More than I ever thought possible," he said, bending to kiss her once more as their guests continued to applaud.

The ceremony had been perfect, and not because of the flawless weather or beautiful decorations, but because it truly reflected who they were as a couple.

As they moved through the crowd accepting congratulations, Bennett caught Clara's eye at the keyboard. She smiled and nodded about the note he had sent earlier. Later, during the reception, they would announce the official naming of the Whitman Gazebo. But for now, the moment belonged to him and Danielle, to the promises they had made before friends and family, and the life they would build together on their beloved island.

CHAPTER 13

The community center had been transformed for the reception. Tables were arranged around a dance floor in the middle, and thousands of little lights created a starlit effect overhead. There were clusters of orchids and sea glass that decorated each table, complemented by candles and hurricane lamps.

Danielle and Bennett made their entrance to enthusiastic applause. The ceremony had been everything they'd hoped for - meaningful, personal, and a true reflection of their relationship. Now it was time to celebrate with the community that had brought them together in the first place.

After their first dance to a piece Clara had composed specifically for the occasion, dinner was served. Esther and her team had outdone themselves, creating a menu that showcased all of the local seafood and seasonal produce. Conversation flowed along with champagne as the room filled with laughter and animated conversations.

Midway through the meal, Eddie stood to offer the first toast. Initially, he seemed a little nervous, but then he found his footing and spoke from his heart.

"I've known Bennett since he had the crazy idea to build this retirement community on an undeveloped island," he said, smiling. "Most people thought it wouldn't work, that it was far too isolated and too unconventional an idea. But Bennett had this vision of creating not just housing, but a true community where people could age with dignity and purpose."

He turned and looked at Danielle. "And then this amazing woman arrived. Initially, just as temporary medical staff, I figured she'd leave just like everybody else had. I remember Bennett calling her, quote, 'the most stubborn, opinionated health care provider he'd ever met' after their first week working together. Those of us who knew Bennett recognized his tone immediately—he was already falling for her, even if he didn't know it yet."

Laughter rippled through the reception as Bennett shook his head, smiling.

"But what makes these two so perfect together isn't just their love for each other, although anybody can plainly see that. It's their shared commitment to this island and the people here. They've put their hearts into making Wisteria Island not just a place to live, but a place where everyone belongs."

He raised his glass. "To Bennett and Danielle. May your marriage be as strong as the foundation of this island, and as beautiful as the community you've built together."

Everybody echoed the toast and clinked glasses as Danielle leaned over to kiss Bennett's cheek.

Dinner continued, and Morty approached the microphone wearing his lavender suit again.

"Ladies and gentlemen," he announced with theatrical flair, "Bennett and Danielle have a special announcement to make."

They both rose, Bennett keeping Danielle's hand firmly in his as they took center stage.

"First of all, we want to thank everyone for being a part of our special day," Bennett said. "Wisteria Island isn't just the place we met—it's where we found our family."

He looked around the room at all of the residents

who had become so much more than just neighbors or patients of Danielle's.

"The gazebo where we exchanged our vows today is going to remain as a permanent addition to the island, and we've decided to name it in honor of someone whose music and friendship have meant so much to us, especially during the last few weeks of planning our wedding."

Danielle took over the speech. "The Whitman Gazebo will stand as a tribute to Clara and her late husband, Robert, whose legacy in music will continue to inspire us all."

Clara was seated at a table near the small stage. She smiled as Bennett spoke. Dorothy sat beside her and reached over to squeeze her hand.

"Also," Bennett said, "we've established a small endowment to ensure that the gazebo will host regular musical performances for this island community, and Clara has graciously agreed to serve as the artistic director for this program."

Everybody clapped, and Clara found herself blinking back tears as residents walked by her table to congratulate her on the news. The unexpected honor touched her deeply—not just the naming of the gazebo, but the opportunity to bring music to the island in an ongoing way. Robert would have loved this, she thought. He always believed music belonged everywhere, not just in concert halls.

As the celebratory atmosphere continued, Cecilia made her way to Clara's table in her elegant dress.

"That was a lovely gesture from Bennett and Danielle," she said, taking an empty seat, "and so well deserved. Your music today was absolutely beautiful."

"Thank you," Clara said. "It means a great deal to me."

"And I understand completely," Cecilia said. "When we lose someone we love, having their name live on—well, it matters."

Dorothy returned from the dance floor, slightly breathless after being whirled around by Morty.

"I swear that man has the energy of someone half his age," she said, fanning herself. "Cecilia, you should try dancing with him. It's positively invigorating."

"I don't dance," Cecilia said quickly.

Dorothy arched an elegant eyebrow. "Oh, nonsense. Everyone dances at weddings. It's actually mandatory, I think."

Clara watched with amusement as Dorothy somehow persuaded the dignified epidemiologist onto the dance floor, just as the band began a lively number. Cecilia moved stiffly at first, but then relaxed under Dorothy's encouraging guidance.

Danielle and Bennett were making their rounds in the room. When they reached Clara, Bennett leaned down to kiss her cheek.

"I hope our speech wasn't too overwhelming."

She shook her head. "It was a beautiful gesture, and I'm deeply honored."

"The gazebo wouldn't exist without you," Danielle said. "Your music was so inspiring in much of the design."

"Besides," Bennett said with a smile, "who better to oversee a music program in a gazebo than a world-class conductor?"

Clara smiled. "Hardly world-class anymore, but I'll do my best to bring beautiful music to the island."

"To your island," Danielle said. "You're a part of Wisteria now, Clara—for as long as you want to be."

The reception continued into the evening, and as it shifted from a formal celebration to more relaxed enjoyment, Bennett found himself momentarily alone as Danielle was swept onto the dance floor by Morty. It promised to be an enthusiastic interpretation of a classic disco song.

"She looks very happy," a voice said over his shoulder.

Bennett turned to find Cecilia holding a glass of champagne.

"I hope so," he said. "That's all I want for her—just true happiness."

Cecilia studied him. "You know, when Danielle first told me about you, I have to admit I was skeptical. A wealthy tech entrepreneur who built an island—it sounded like a lot of red flags to me."

Bennett laughed. "I can see how that might have been a little concerning."

"But watching you together… You truly see her, don't you? Not just her beauty or her intelligence, but who she really is inside."

"From the moment she arrived on Wisteria," he said, "even when she was telling me everything I was doing wrong."

Cecilia smiled. "Well, she comes by that honestly. Her father and I were never one-time mentors either." She placed her hand on Bennett's arm. "Take care of each other. That's all that really matters in the end. Not the careers or the achievements, but how well you care for the people you love."

"I'm starting to realize that myself. I will," Bennett said.

Cecilia nodded. "And I expect you to bring her to New York occasionally. You know, just because she's found paradise on the island doesn't mean she should forget civilization entirely."

"We'll visit," Bennett said. "And you're always welcome here anytime, for as long as you'd like."

"Well, I may take you up on that," she said. "I find I've become rather fond of this peculiar little community of yours, especially now that my daughter is first lady, so to speak."

She moved away to join Dorothy and Clara at their table.

Bennett felt a sense of satisfaction, not just because the wedding had gone off without a hitch, but because the community had come together to celebrate with them. When Wisteria Island had only been his vision—a place where people could age with dignity, purpose, and connection—he had never imagined this. He knew the vision had actually been realized beyond his wildest hopes and dreams.

But now, at the center of it all, was Danielle.

As she made her way back to him, slightly out of breath, with Morty still dancing behind her, he smiled.

"Having fun, Mrs. Alexander?" he asked, pulling her into his arms.

"Oh, the most fun," she said, leaning in to kiss him. "Though I think I need to request slower songs from now on because Morty's idea of dancing is completely aerobic."

He laughed and held her close. "Whatever you want, today and always."

They swayed together as the band shifted to a slower song, lost in their own world for a moment, despite the crowd around them.

"Are you ever going to tell me where we're going on our honeymoon?" Danielle asked, laughing.

Bennett smiled down at her. "Where's the fun in that? I thought I'd blindfold you on the way to the airport terminal and then…"

She lightly punched him in the stomach. "You'd better not!"

"Okay, fine. You and I are going on a two-week adventure around Italy, France, and Spain."

Danielle's mouth dropped open. "Seriously?"

"Seriously. We're staying in castles and villas. We're eating all the food. I hope to come back ten pounds heavier."

She smiled. "You're already spoiling me, Mr. Alexander. How will you ever top this honeymoon?"

He hugged her tightly. "I don't know, but I'm sure going to have fun trying, Mrs. Alexander."

EPILOGUE

The waves lapped gently at Wisteria Island's shore as Danielle stood on the deck of her cottage, watching the winter sunset paint the sky in breathtaking shades of pink and gold. Six months had passed since her perfect wedding day, and the memory still brought a smile to her face. The beautiful gazebo stood off in the distance, a testament to her wonderful new marriage.

She absently placed her hand on her abdomen, still flat but harboring the most precious secret. Three pregnancy tests had confirmed what she'd begun to suspect two weeks ago. She and Bennett were going to have a baby.

The sliding door opened behind her, and

Bennett's arms wrapped around her, his chin resting on top of her head.

"That's a beautiful sunset," he said.

"Perfect timing," Danielle said, leaning back against his chest, "and everybody should be arriving soon."

They'd invited their closest friends for dinner—Clara, Dorothy, Morty, and Cecilia, who was visiting from New York for the weekend. Her mother's health issues before the wedding had led to some significant life changes. She addressed her hypertension and exhaustion, and then Cecilia shocked everyone by cutting back on her academic schedule to establish a telehealth consultancy focused on rural healthcare access. Even more surprising was her decision to split her time between Manhattan and Wisteria Island. She maintained a cottage just down the path from Danielle and Bennett's home.

"So did you tell anybody why we're hosting this dinner?" Bennett asked.

"Just that we want to celebrate our six-month anniversary? No one suspects a thing."

Bennett turned her to face him. "I still can't believe it. We're going to be parents. You're going to be a mom, and I'm going to be a dad, and all these people on the island will be grandparents."

"Are you terrified?" she asked with a smile.

"Absolutely," he said, "but happier than I've ever been."

They could hear the sound of animated conversation on the front porch, including Morty's distinctive boisterous laugh and Dorothy's smoky voice as they made their way up the path.

"Showtime," Bennett said, quickly kissing her before opening the front door.

Morty walked in in his typical fashion, a bottle of champagne in one hand and a brightly wrapped package in the other. He wore a vibrant purple and green sweater that somehow complemented his orange bow tie without causing visual distress.

"Happy semi-anniversary to the most beautiful couple on Wisteria Island," he said, thrusting the bottle in Bennett's direction. "Six months of wedded bliss deserves proper celebration."

Dorothy walked in, elegant as always, wearing a silk tunic and wide-legged pants.

"Oh my goodness, he's been planning this celebration for weeks," she said to Danielle, rolling her eyes. "Apparently, half-year anniversaries are now mandatory occasions."

"Well, any reason for a party," Danielle said, hugging them both.

Clara arrived next and brought a platter of delicate pastries.

"I brought these from Esther," she said. "She sent her regrets, but couldn't leave because of the dinner rush."

"And here comes the distinguished Dr. Wright," Bennett said as Cecilia walked up the cottage stairs, looking stylish in her pink cashmere sweater and tailored slacks.

Danielle was getting used to seeing her mother in more casual attire. The health scare before the wedding had changed more than just Cecilia's work schedule. It had softened some of her sharp edges.

"Am I late?" she asked, kissing Danielle's cheek.

"Right on time," Bennett said. "We're just about to open some wine."

"Oh, none for me, thank you," Danielle said. "I'm still recovering from a little stomach bug."

Her mother's eyes narrowed slightly, but she didn't say anything and took her own glass.

Dinner was a lively affair with Morty telling them tales of the island's latest talent show and talking about how they might want to close down that little section of nude beach. Some people had been traumatized by seeing old Mr. Wisely without his clothes on.

Clara shared news of the spring concert series she was planning for the Whitman Gazebo. And of course, Dorothy gave colorful commentary about recent film club selections that she'd organized for the residents.

"You know, I still think that introducing octogenarians to Fellini was an educational choice," she said when Morty accused her of traumatizing the film club.

"Gladys had nightmares for a week," he said. "Next time, maybe we stick with Audrey Hepburn."

"Coward," Dorothy said, rolling her eyes.

Cecilia had been quietly observing Danielle throughout the meal.

"You've barely touched your food, darling. Is that stomach bug still bothering you?" She put emphasis on the words *stomach bug*.

All eyes turned to Danielle, who exchanged a quick glance with Bennett. They had hoped to wait until dessert, but her mother had sharp medical instincts. Bennett reached for her hand under the table and gave it a supportive squeeze.

"Actually," Danielle said, feeling flutters in her stomach that had nothing to do with a baby, "it's not exactly a bug." She smiled. "We're pregnant. We're going to have a baby."

A momentary silence was broken by Morty's squeal of delight. He leapt from his chair.

"A baby! The first Wisteria Island baby. I mean, nobody else on Wisteria Island could have a baby. All the eggs are too old. But anyway, this is magnificent news. Oh my goodness, we have so much to plan. A nursery, a baby shower. Do you know if it's a boy or a girl yet? We need to start thinking about color schemes."

Dorothy removed her reading glasses. "Congratulations, my dears. When are you due?"

"Late summer," Danielle said. "August, we think."

"Well, I'm sorry that Morty has already broken the child's ears by screaming so loud. But again, congratulations."

Clara reached across the table and squeezed Danielle's hand. "What wonderful news! You're going to be such great parents."

Danielle turned to her mother, who had remained quiet. "Mom?"

Cecilia couldn't hide the emotion in her eyes. "A grandchild? I'm going to be a grandmother."

"The most glamorous grandmother on the Eastern Seaboard," Bennett said, "and we were hoping you might want to spend even more time on the island after the baby arrives. He or she should get to know their grandmother."

"Oh, I'd like that very much," Cecilia said. She rose and hugged Danielle. "I'm so happy for you, dear. So very happy."

The rest of the evening passed in a blur of excitement and plans, mostly from Morty's side. He immediately started sketching out nursery designs on napkins, and Dorothy offered a list of appropriate baby names drawn from the golden age of cinema. Clara promised to compose a lullaby especially for the baby, of course. And Cecilia, in a moment of unexpected sentimentality, said that she intended to teach her grandchild French, *"as soon as they have sufficient cognitive development"*.

Later, when everyone departed with hugs and more congratulations, Danielle and Bennett stood on the deck once more, watching stars emerge over the ocean.

"That went really well," he said, wrapping his arms around her from behind, his hands resting protectively on her stomach.

"Better than I expected. Did you see my mother's face? I don't think I've ever seen her speechless before."

"We've created a miracle."

"Well, we've created a lot of them," Danielle said. "This baby, our marriage, this wonderful community we call home." She turned in his arms and faced him. "When I first came to this island, I was running away from embarrassment and heartbreak, convinced I could never trust a man again, or really anyone. And now look at what we've built."

"Look at us," he echoed. "We built our family on this island, and we're going to make it even bigger," he said, touching her midsection.

She rested her head against his chest and listened to the steady rhythm of his heartbeat. In a few months, their baby would join this unique island family and grow up surrounded not by just the parents who loved them, but by an extended family of honorary grandparents who each had wisdom and love to share.

Morty would teach their child creativity and being unapologetic about who you are. Dorothy would definitely impart some dramatic flair—over and above what Morty would provide. Clara would bring music and show them how to find beauty after loss. And her mother, Cecilia, would make sure her child had culture, education, and the confidence to stand their ground in any circumstance.

"Are you still happy?" Bennett murmured against her hair.

"Completely. Are you?"

"More than I ever dreamed was possible."

As they stood together in starlight, Danielle felt such a sense of belonging. Wisteria Island had given her everything she never even knew she wanted: a home, a purpose, a husband who understood her, and now a child. The island's gentle sounds surrounded them - night birds calling, waves against the shore, and distant laughter from the community center where the weekly game night was in full swing. These were the sounds their child would grow up hearing.

Danielle placed her hand over Bennett's, where it rested on her stomach. There was no bump yet, no visible mark to show the miracle growing inside of her, but they both felt it—their expansion of their love into something new and limitless.

She knew there were challenges ahead: sleepless nights, childhood illnesses, worries of parenthood. But they would face them together, supported by their remarkable community.

And to Danielle, that was the greatest gift of all.

Did you know I have a private Facebook reader group with over 25,000 members? We have a ton of fun in there every day, so if you'd like to engage with me personally and meet other great people, join us at https://www.facebook.com/groups/RachelReaders

Made in United States
Orlando, FL
22 June 2025

62300139R00136